Mi Books

Fiction
Short Story Collection
©2019

Like Garden Eyes

Dedicated to

My Mom, Annie Adufutse

My Dad, M. William Adufutse

My Sister, Adrianna Adufutse

and

Sandra Cisneros
whose short story book The House on Mango Street
I fell in love with in 12th grade

Like Garden Eyes

Like Garden Eyes
Table of Contents

Samasi's Secret	7
Adaptation	65
The Reapers	75
The Other Woman	87
Dachelle, Dachelle...Dachelle From Hell	93
Blood	101
Can't Help Everyone	111
Adaptation 2	119
Dandelion Werewolf	125
No Other	135
Sacrifice	141
It Doesn't Always End The Way It Starts	149
Shamar & His Wife	153
Lost & Found	167
The Ruse's Veneration	209
Young, Futile Old Girl	213
The Cult	217
Ishia	229
Like Garden Eyes	235

Like Garden Eyes

Samasi's Secret

"Hey! Good to see you," Samasi's first and ex husband, a lanky, lame and too awkward looking for a Black dude growing up in a Detroit hood, greeted walking over completely disregarding her new husband. For all of a second Samasi (Suh-mah-see) looked him in the face and noticed his pride and regret. You could bet your bottom dollar he wasn't expecting this: a new, shorter dude with a baby sucking on a pacifier in his right arm and the almost two years old little one standing between Samasi and her new husband holding Samasi's hand. This first husband always thought he knew her type and *clearly* this new brotha was not it. She'd always liked tall dudes. And Samasi? Brown skinned, she was absolutely stunning as ever--still looked as good as she did on their wedding day and still had that body, not too much but not too little in all the right places.

    Samasi who almost everyone only ever calls Samah, gives him the stiffest, fakest smile possible, nods her head once at him in place of a hello, pushes her two year old daughter in front of her and keeps it moving. *Damn festival!* Samah thinks to herself. Until now she'd done well to avoid him and all free to the public events she knew he was too cheap to miss out 'parking lot pimpin' at.

"Is that him?" James asks a bit indifferently. James knows what he himself is capable of and in no way or shape is threatened. He had always wanted Samah even though at first her feelings weren't mutual. He went away to school, had all the single life fun he could've possibly wanted and *still* ended up getting his girl once he came back. The way he sees it, ole boy only made it that much easier.

"Um-hm," she responds not about to say anything else about that fool and James knew not to ask anything else about it. Besides, James already knew enough to know he himself had considerable leverage. The ex had been too scared to get it up the first night and had punched her in the eye because he hadn't believed her job let her off late a month after the honeymoon--definitely a crazy ass bastard. Biting an envelope and spitting it out at her when he couldn't control his temper and how he was always drunk were just a few of the things Samah didn't ever wanna think about again. But. If all that led her to James, then so be it.

"I love you," James says as he touches her right elbow with his left hand right before grabbing their daughter Taemar's hand.

Samah looks over at him and smiles. "Oooh. Over there—there are some seats."

"Aright. It sucks that we couldn't find the folding chairs." The seating is not so clean and they are both wearing cream.

"We're not gonna be here that long, anyway, right?"

"Nah, I wanna get something to eat in a lil bit. You wanna try that new spot in Royal Oak, Comos or Anita's Kitchen?"

"Anita's kitchen is cool with me." James is always considerate when it comes to Samah. Even back in high school. She shoulda dated him in the first place instead of that goddamn Jeffery. What a loser. James, who at the time was a senior, had chased her all while she was in tenth grade and even asked her to his prom. We never seem to like the ones we get along with best at first.

Jeffery had visited her church one time and somehow found his way to a seat near her and was so persistent for the next year she somehow found herself saying "I Do" completely unsure weeks before, during and after their wedding.

The baby, the boy, starts to get testy for a minute but James knows the cry--breast milk bottle time. Samah wouldn't mind breast feeding Baye right there but James is way too in love with the love of his life turned wife to even bear thinking about anyone catching a glimpse of what's his.

"Ooh. Listen to the music Tae," Samah encourages Taemar who is already in love with jazz. Taemar smiles back really wide and gets comfortable on her mommy's lap.

"This festival has a really good lineup," James notes. Eclectic pretty girls of all races are out but James couldn't care less. If Samah even begins to *look* like she's not having a good time—they're out.

"You ready?" James asks after almost an hour.

"Yeah, you mind going in that vintage store for a minute?"

"Aright," James responds.

But Taemar is getting sleepy so they head to the car and Anita's Kitchen on Woodward for dinner.

"You know what? I wish we woulda done sushi," James states. With exception of Samah and the kids, James is never completely satisfied with anything. If it woulda been sushi, then he woulda been complaining about not going to Anita's Kitchen. But that never bothers her. It all comes down to a good backrub and a little fun after the kids are tucked in to get him out of the his normal cranky disposition.

"He always makes that face." Samah laughs at Baye who, for a seven month old, seems to understand everything they say. Baye continues laughing as James makes fun of his mother's latest beef with his aunt Denise.

"But you know what?--I see where both of them are coming from… I like your momma and your aunt," Samah says.

"Yeah, but they act too crazy sometimes. Both of them take everything too far," James replies.

Samah listens and only smirks back. She never gets involved in her own family's beefs let alone his. That has always been her secret when it comes to getting along with people—staying out of everyone else's business.

"You know steak is kinda heavy to go to sleep on, baby," Samah reminds James.

"Yeah, but I'ma work it off before I go to sleep." They exchange knowing glances as James swaps a few bites of steak for her baked salmon and rice pilaf. Taemar isn't really hungry and is only picking at the kiddie chicken fingers and fruit Samah figured she wasn't going to eat anyway.

"This song always makes me think about you," James says in the car on the way home listening to Josh Milan's song "You're Body." He reached for Samah's hand and kisses it and the minute they get to the crib and pull the car into the garage, he puts the kids straight to bed--no bedtime stories tonight.

James heads for the shower where Samah is waiting for him to slide in next to her. He pulls her closer and kisses her softly and deeply, circling soap into the ticklish spots on her back and thighs. She giggles back in response. "Man, I love you." He sighs against the side of her face.

"I love—ah—I love you, too," she moans as he completely becomes one with her in the place within her that is his. "Ah—um, baby." James definitely knows his wife's body. They rinse off still not satisfied and rushed to their bedroom.

"Why ma pussy always godda taste so sweet, hunh? …Got uh nigga addicted and shit," James mutters doing alphabets on Samah's second set of lips. In a few seconds his mouth will be completely covered in glistening pussy juice.

Samah slides over and rolls on top of James simultaneously returning the favor--69. Right before he busts, Samah fucks him real hard, swerving her hips reverse cowgirl style, watching her breasts bounce in the mirror to the beat James and her are making. Samah knows how to make James bust a nut within seconds, which comes in handy on nights like tonight when she is starting to get tired and knows James will be trying to go for three more hours. Really, all she has to do is say his name long enough and it's all over for him—they'll be seconds away from going to sleep in each other's arms. And the funny thing about it is, no matter what, even when Samah tosses and turns in her sleep, James tosses in his sleep right along with her. She always wakes up to him holding her.

The next morning James steps into the kitchen. Samah hands him a plate--lightly toasted bagel with Philly cream cheese, Morning Star veggie sausages, scrambled eggs and orange juice she's mixed with fresh strawberry and limes juiced in the blender. She wonders if he'll catch the heart she patted with the butter knife in the cream cheese. He does and looks up and smiles.

Just looking at him and the way he looks all extra calm in the morning makes her smile right back.

"Aright, babe. I'll see you at six. Nnevah (Nuh-vah) is supposed to be stopping by to drop off those invitations for ma's retirement party around three."

"Okay. Love you," Samah responds.

"Love you, too." James plants a kiss on her lips even though she hadn't brushed her teeth yet and her breath is a bit harsh.

In a second Taemar will be up and making enough noise to wake up Baye.

Samah does a pilates workout with that lady instructor on public television with Taemar trying to copy off her while Baye is crawling all over the place content to finally be out of the crib and able to get somewhere on his own.

"Whassup!" Nnevah shows up a little after three. Samah has just gotten back from Partridge Creek mall with the kids.

"Hey, Vah!" Nnevah is one of James's oldest homeboys and Samah's favorite out of all of them—which, all of them are good people. All they ever do is hang out on Fridays and go to the DIA and Inner State Gallery, out to eat at Union Street or hit up the movies in Royal Oak all coupled up, watch the sport's games, compete to see who's the coolest and listen to music. But two of the girls, the chicks Samah's known a long time and still does not really care to get to know better, kind of annoy her. They act like fashion gurus even though they're always dressed in gaudy goodwill-looking shit and look terrible.

"Listen to this! Wait a minute—y'all moved Alexa?

"Yeah, The Echo's in the basement. It kinda freaks me out. Seems like the government is taping into our house now."

"I know, right? 1984,"Vah responds before going downstairs. Within a few seconds the surround system is blasting.

"JDavey?"

"Yep, the one from a while ago. You should check out the Ben Khan station on Pandora but I've been listening to Nina Simone live, Yuna, Amel Larrieux, Sinead Harnett, Little Dragon and The Philly Symphony Orchestra. Check 'em out."

"That JDavey's *hot*. I always felt their stuff. I want to hear the rest of the list." Vah and Samah are the only two out of their thirty-something clique with the exact same taste in music. "Hold on, I'll be right back--nap time for

13

these kids. There's food in there." She nods towards the kitchen at Nnevah while picking up Baye who would rather slowly crawl up the stairs with the speed of a baby turtle. "Miss Taemar, come on, honey. It's nap time."

"*Nooooo*, mo*mmy*!"

"Trust, me. One day you're gonna be wishing you could take a nap—especially when you get a job!" A little while ago James had texted her that he needed a nap. And knowing him, he was probably locked in his office taking one right about now, too.

"You want me to go turn the music down?" Vah calls after her.

"No!" When Samasi comes back down she adds, "Ung-uh. One thing you learn when you have kids is to leave the music up real loud when it's sleepytime. Otherwise you end up not being able to do anything because every little sound will wake 'em up. Ung-uh, I don't have time for all of that."

Vah chuckles. Vah is actually very handsome. Six two, a nice smile, cream skinned, slender but muscular with thick black curly hair and big brown eyes. He looks like the type of dude that would always be on a runway and does not at all look like he fits in with the rest of the Afrocentric, artsy bohemian crew.

"You *made* this?" he points at the Greek salad Samah's fixed for lunch.

"Y*eah*!" she answers like he is retarded.

"Dang. I can't even get Justina to *order* carryout." He laughs but is dead serious. Justina is the classic glam girl. What did he expect? But of course, Samah will keep any opinions like these to herself. Besides. Justina is the only chick that hangs with the crew who doesn't act real funny towards her.

Samah's great-grandma taught her how to cook everything from the old schooled catfish dipped in cornmeal to three layered pound cakes. Thank God! Samah's mother was a vegan who only kept unsalted crackers around the house and watered everything including the herbal tea down—sodium, she said, was the main attraction for hypertension—that was her excuse. But really, everyone in the family said Samah's mom just didn't know how to cook and was a Black, sober hippie. Hippie mama and southern great-granny, Samah can do anything from homemade butter biscuits and tender barbecue ribs with her great-granny's special sauce, ox tails to spinach quiche, grape leaves and Tabouli.

Samah wishes to tell Vah this but decides not to. "So what are you about to do?"

"Um…nothing really. I'm off today, so I'm chillin'." Nnevah owns his own club promotional company and, although he isn't the richest cat around, he is doing pretty okay for himself. He's always hooking everybody up with free concert tickets in and out of town. This year they are all supposed to be going to the Cincinnati Jazz Festival together.

As usual, Vah will end up chilling and staying over for dinner and won't answer any of Justina's calls. The chick is really driving him crazy. That's all he's been talking to Samah about for the last hour, which is starting to drive Samah *crazy*.

"Man, it's always the fine ones that act crazy. See. Look at this." He shows her the seventh repeat text from Justina written in all large caps: **WHERE THA HELL R U????**

"Correction, *I'm* fine and *I'm not* crazy," Samah protest.

"Yeah, my bad. You cool, you cool. I'm a lil jealous of my mans. You're like the only woman around nowadays that actually know how to keep a house clean and shit."

"You think that's all women are supposed to know how to do?"

He sighs. "You know I'm not saying that. You're educated and have hobbies worth mentioning and shit. All Justina knows how to do is whine about shit all the time and spend money."

James is walking in the door and straight up not liking Nnevah being in his house with all the Jodeci and Amerie music playing. This is, what?--the fifth time within the last month homeboy's been straight up at his crib chillin' like he lives there when James comes home from work. All James wants to do is head upstairs to the bathroom then come down and have dinner with his family--a Nnevah-free dinner--with his wife and kids. He is doing very well this evening conveying his point with his extra grumpiness. Why did he even tell this Negro to bring the invitations over? He could have just gotten them after he got off work.

"Baby, could you gimme that, please?" Samah points towards the pitcher of cucumber water on the table.

James rolls his eyes and grunts slightly before lifting the pitcher and pouring cucumber water into her glass.

"Baby, Vah played some throwback JDavey tracks... They're hot to death."

James stares at Vah real hard. *This nigga is always trying to put my girl up on shit.*

"Well...I'm gonna go—I'm gonna go load the dishwasher," Samah declares finally realizing James' attitude.

"Yeah, I better get rollin'. I'll help you clean up—it's the least I can do in exchange for dinner. You know I don't get home cooked meals around my way." Vah snickers.

James gives Vah a look that means, *nigga you bedda not* and James interjects, "Nah, it's cool. Have a good night, man."

"Baby? It's *just Nnevah*. Why you godda be actin' all funny like that? He could feel it, baby. I don't get mad when you hang out with Chrissette—*or* Renee..." And Samah really couldn't stand Renee. Polish Renee who tried so hard to act Black it was a shame. Over pronouncing words like "naw" making it sound more like "nah-aa-ow"—like a country bumbkin with a stuttering problem.

"Yeah, well it's different with them. They don't be all up in the crib every fuckin' time you come home and shit!"

Samah pauses *Everybody Loves Raymond* on Fire TV Stick's Crackle. "Hold on! Correction! They don't do that!—ungh-uh, no! What *they do* is invite you over all the time *without* me!"

"No they don't!"

"Well how come every time you go over there it's on the last minute tip, then? And I'm *noooo where* around!"

James smirks and tries to take the remote from Samah, enjoying the fact that she actually seems jealous for a change. But he didn't mean for her to catch him smirking.

"OOOh! Oh! *Oooh*! I see!" Samah is on the way to doing something real stupid. Something she's never pulled before. For all these times James has hung out with his quote unquote female best friends, to really piss him off.

She goes to the front closet, grabs her jacket and goes out to the car in the garage and calls Nnevah on her phone. "Why is James trippin' on me?" She doesn't go any further.

"Whassup?" Nnevah inquires.

She sighs and smacks her lips. "He's just pissing me off."

"Man, come on, na. He's cool. Y'all love each other. You know I ain't abouta dig on my mans… Anyway, y'all going to that Jose James concert or what?"

"I don't know…I think James said he might wanna go… What other stuff is coming up?"

"I'm going to New York next week for this Monique Bingham gig. I'll let y'all know whassup with that soon."

"That's cool. Aye—have you seen that new reality show with all the one hit wonders on it? You know I don't watch TV all like that but I like it," Samah says.

"Man, that's female shit. And another thing I ain't tryin' to catch is that *Black Ink Crew* or that *Real Housewives* shit," Nnevah responds.

"*Oh, what-ever*! You were all in on that *Flavor of Love* nonsense back in the day. What woman is gonna let a man take her to KFC on television and then gonna try to sleep with him? And did you see how Flavor-Flav was eating when they were at dinner? *Gross*! If you can stand to watch *that*, then you should be able to watch *Black Ink Creew*!"

"Man, whatever. That ain't reality. Ain't no man gonna go on television and cry and fight on a dating game over a chick like that!"

"None of it's real anyway. They're nothing but paid actors," Samah replies.

"That's why I work on counting my paper. Fuck, fuck, fuck watching other motherfuckas make theirs," Vah sings it in this real funny way that makes Samah start laughing--laughing before she remembers she'd better get back in the house.

"Aright, Vah. I'll talk to you later. It's getting late. I've godda give the kids their baths and go make up with my Honey Bunny."

"Peace, Massie," Vah states and it weirds her out for a second. The only other person to ever call her that was her dad.

When she goes back inside, James is already giving Baye his bath. Taemar is in the hallway playing with the shiny pink baton she begged at the toy store for, jumping over it and then stomping on it.

James doesn't say anything to Samah until after they finish reading Taemar her nighttime story.

He looks at his wife long and hard before going downstairs, going in her purse, punching in their anniversary, which is the code, and looks thru the calls on her phone.

"Nnevah," he says quietly.

"Yep. My grandma used to say: what's good for the goose is good for the gander."

They just look at each other for a couple of seconds, him in the dining room, her in the living room.

"Okay. I see your point. I'm sorry. How 'bout I won't hang out with them anymore unless you come with?" he proposes finally.

Samah debates long and hard on if she even truly cares and decides that she does. "Okay."

"I'ma check dat nigga Nnevah, though."

"Should I check Renee and Chrissette, too? If you check Nnevah, then I need to light into them, too."

"Okay, okay. I'll leave it alone. But I don't wanna see that nigga chillin' all up in my house like that when I'm not here anymore."

Samah goes into the bathroom and starts wrapping her hair and gets in the shower. When she gets in bed, James rolls over on top of her. "Come here, baby." She shouldn't have even put the nightgown on. It's off within seconds and James is rolling the tip of his dick all over her clit. "Baby? I really love you…" Samah knows that what is he really saying is *You're mine! And I was wrong as hell for hanging out with Chrissette and Renee now that I know how it feels—but I don't wanna flat-out admit it.*

"Did you see what Chrissette's wearing?" Samah asks James after they pull out of the gas station. They're on the way to

Cincinnati trailing Vah and Justine, Chrissette and The Drake and Cardboard Man, dubbed that because of his cardboard art designs, which sounds awful but are actually phenomenal.

"Yeah, that's my girl but she do be on some wack shit sometimes."

They both laugh.

"I'm just glad we didn't take them up on all riding together in The Drake's truck," Samah says.

"Yeah, me, too. The Drake is the fartiest muthafuka I ever met," James responds.

But Samah is glad not only because of that. Things have been really weird with her and Vah for the last couple of months. Whenever they all go out lately, they both steer clear of each other and avoid all eye contact and James seems way happier with things that way. Samah knows James said some shit to him even though he promised he wouldn't. But. James is acting funny towards his once "two female best friends" in return so she guesses it's even-- except she missed not having to find new, good music. Hours spent skipping songs on Pandora when Vah would have put her up on the best tracks in seconds or come over and just play them on Echo. Plus, Vah would've been able to tell her all about each band or the singer's background—how they got started, how many albums they did before finally being discovered—all of that type of stuff.

James has stopped making Samasi call his mother to check on the little ones every hour now that they've finally arrived in Cincinnati. Once they check into the Marriot, James showers and goes out with the fellas to get drunk.

Samah changes too and decides to go to the nearby mall to look for a pair of black heels to match the black lace jumper she's planning on wearing to the concert tomorrow. Lately, all they have at the mall are those darn chunky heels that Samah feels are not at all sexy. She did that style back in the day, and when that happens--when you've already done a style, when it comes back around it's usually hard to get with.

She grabs her tablet so she can get back into the Octavia Butler book she's been reading, puts it in her purse and almost forgets the keycard but goes back in right before the door has a chance to lock shut.

"Samah, Samah! Wait up for me!" She turns around in the middle of pressing the down elevator button to Justina bouncing her way towards her.

"Where're you off to?" Justina asks.

"Ooh…to window shop maybe." Samah hesitates. She hasn't had any time just for herself in the last week and really isn't looking for company. James going out with the boys was big plus. Husbands and wives needed a break from each other once in a while.

"Oh. I'll go with you."

"…You aren't going out with the crew?"

"Girl, no! I need a break from Nnevah. I almost didn't come on this trip with him. He's been really getting on my nerves lately," Justina informs her.

TMI, Samah thinks already regretting not leaving a few seconds earlier so as to miss out on Justina, Justina the Drama Queena—more channels of drama than Hulu.

"He totally ignores me! All he ever does is go out with The Drake, hang out at the clubs every night of the week—well, except when he hangs out with you guys! He ignores *the hell* outta me! Then, he's always monitoring what I buy and stuff! I *work*! I don't know who told him his name was on the checks Michigan First Credit Union issues Justina Morgan every Friday for the last four years—before I even met a Nnevah Taylor!" she sighed. "Men!—You feel me?"

Samah smiles politely, still shocked Justina's got a job. First time she's heard of it.

"Ooh-oh-oh! I'm hungry—wait!" Justina says, stopping, turning around and walking into a trendy looking restaurant across from the Marriot.

"You mind if we check a few boutiques out really quick—that's where I was headed. And James told me to order at the Marriot and to charge the room. You wanna just order something when we get back?" Samah asks.

"James *told* you?" Justina frowns and gives Samah a look of absolute disapproval.

"*Yes*," Samah replies in a way that also serves as a *You got a problem with that*? Samah didn't work and didn't have to. And she had no problem with James telling her to charge lunch to the hotel. She had three hundred dollars in her purse James had just given her.

"Okay, okay! I won't be that long. You mind going to eat with me? *Please*? I hate going out by myself—I think it looks *sooo* pitiful to see a woman out at a restaurant all by herself—don't you?" Justina asks.

"I do it all the time. Sometimes I take the kids to visit my parents and go out to the movies and out to eat alone. It doesn't bother me," Samah responds.

All Justina orders to eat is a salad but she has two martinis.

"Can we have the bill please," Samah requests in a rush.

The server places it in front of Samah. She hands it over to Justina who is now fumbling, fumbling and *still* fumbling for her credit card in a purse so small, if she drops an earring back in it, she'll find it in seconds. "Dang, it! Samah, can I borrow thirty dollars? Well, twenty-five—I'll just have to skip the tip." He shouldn'ta picked waitressing if he was trying to get rich!"

"Who said *I* had money?" Samah is pissed. She hadn't even ordered anything! Not even a glass of water!

"I'll get Vah to give it back to you tonight—I promise."

As they leave out of the restaurant three well-dressed brothas in suits also on their way out rush to open the doors for them.

"How are you ladies doing this afternoon?" the finest one asks. Samah crosses her arms and purposely exposes her wedding ring. He starts paying extra attention to Justina who is soaking it up.

"We're good. We just got in town and we're looking for something fun to get into tonight…" Justina says.

"Oh. Where are you from?" he asks.

"Detroit."

"Yeah? How long are you gonna be in town?"

"We really aren't gonna be here for that long…tonight's like the only night I have free…" Justina smiles in a siren manner.

"Well…my office just handed out tickets to the jazz festival kick off tonight—Kem's gonna be playing, if you'd like to go?" The guy asks.

"Hmm…that sounds…that sounds nice," Justina says like she's in deep thought.

"My office is right across the street—J. D. Powell & Powell. Jason Powell Junior—pleasure to meet you." They shake hands. Though the brotha is very fine—clean *and* dapper—Justina is straight outta control--wilin' out for real.

"I'm Justina." Seconds later she opens her tiny Chanel bag, pulls out a business card and hands it to him. "Don't tell Nnevah." She giggles and whispers to Samah although the guys are now well out of earshot.

"…You know, what you do is your business but—Vah is like family to me. And he's a really good guy who cares a lot about you… I'm not trying to be judgmental or anything but…" Samasi shakes her head. "Don't put me in the middle of your personal--whatever. I think I'm gonna go back to the hotel." She leaves Justina behind, turns the corner and heads to the mall by herself like she knows she should have done in the first place.

Samah find the exact shoes she had in mind then goes to the bookstore and is flipping thru a book of prayers when James texts her **I luv u**. A call comes thru and interrupts her reply back to him.

"Hey, Samasi. Look. I feel really bad. Can we talk?" Justina asks.

"No," Samasi doesn't hesitate to answer.

"Listen! I know it looks like I'm not right but—well, you know you're the only girl outta the whole crew I can even talk to. I really like you and I don't want you to think I'm like—like I don't care about Nnevah. I do. I *really* do. But you *know* he's been cheating on me for like the last four months of our quote unquote relationship. I wouldn't be shocked if *you done* met the girl before! Samasi, you just don't know what it's like—all this shit Nnevah is putting me thru. Like, I know—I know like it's not cool but—I really love Nnevah and dating other dudes is the only way I can like stay sane. I really hope—I *really* hope you won't say anything… You don't know the entire situation…"

    Samasi pauses before responding. "Vah is a good guy and he really cares about you. *You* need talk to him and tell *him* you think he's cheating—it's stuff like this that causes people to catch HIV. I godda go, Justina."

    James comes in at 2 am totally plastered and doesn't want to do anything but sleep and snore the loud, bubbly kind of snores that sound like planes taking off and vibrate pillows.

    Samah, who doesn't feel like listening to the ruckus or smelling the gin seep thru James's pores at the present moment, decides to go out to the lobby to finish the ebook she's reading. Instead of going down to the lobby, she decides to sit on the floor and hang out in the hallway, to people watch and chill. She is sometimes different like that which is why she fits in with the clique and why she's the perfect match for James who, after the nine to five, is not at all conservative.

    Somebody is fucking but it's not Chrissette and The Drake. Sounds like two really, really old people who like shouting the letter O a million times. "O-O-O-O"-then it stops. Then it begins all over again for a little while longer before the man announces, "I AM COMING! I AM COMING!" like an Irish warlock of the fourteenth century.

Then for sometime instead of reading Samah daydreams about a knitting business she'd like to start. When she stops thinking about how she plans on one day becoming The Knit Queen and hosting a public television show all about knitting, she realizes Nnevah is standing a couple steps away shaking his head at her. "Whatever it is, it must be deep."

"Nah. I'm just thinking about something--that's all. Dreams."

"What dreams you got?" He walks over and sits down next to her on the floor. "Trying to keep up with the record y'all set—a kid every year?" he ask before chuckling. She almost chuckles too but they both stop, realizing it's kind of weird to joke about stuff like that; it's something anyone can clearly notice but something people aren't supposed to let other people know they've noticed. "What'chu thinkin' about?" Nnevah still wants to know.

"Nothing." She shakes her head and dismisses it. "Is it still kinda warm out?"

"Yeah," Nnevah answers.

"I think I'm gonna go for a walk, then."

"By yourself? I'll go with you... I'm like the only one that didn't get tore up tonight," Nnevah says.

"You never drink, anyway."

"Nope. Never. I take that back—one time, back at Eastern. I almost got alcohol poisoning and that was it—I was straight after that...Never picked up a drink since. Damn, Justina's texting me again."

"She in the room?"

"Nah, she went somewhere…"

"Thanks for the tickets, Vah."

"Yep. Come on, you still going for a walk?"

"Uh, no, James might get pissed…" It slips out before she even realizes what she's said.

"Just come down to the lobby with me, then. Chrissette and The Drake are down there."

"Where've you been all day?" Chrissette immediately lights into Samah accusingly but the fellas don't seem to notice.

Samah doesn't look her way or reply. Instead she finishes reading her on her tablet, goes back upstairs and sleeps-in the Saturday morning.

"**Dang, Samasi.** Or *is that* brown skinned hottie Samasi?" The Drake jokes when they meet in the lobby for the Benz van ride to the jazz festival and Cardboard Man and everyone else except Chrissette add compliments to The Drake's comment.

Justina is M.I.A.—supposedly a late summer's flu.

Raheem DeVaugh is up first for the musical throwback set. They're in front row, all except Vah who's somewhere working behind scenes and later, after the concert arranges for them to go back stage to meet Common and Raheem. Samah stares at Common realizing for the first time just how fine the brotha is in real life— that slightly flared nose of his and all.

On Sunday before driving back to Michigan, they do brunch at some spot The Drake wanted to try because they served rattlesnake and frog meat, which *should have* but did not gross anybody out.

That will be the last time for a long time Samah and James get along so well.

And it will bother the mess out of Samah. She'll come up with all type of theories: maybe Justina told Nnevah something about *her* to cover *her* butt; maybe Chrissette was somewhere nearby when Justina was talking to that one lawyer guy and thought she was with it, too; maybe Nnevah said something to James; maybe The Drake did?

But none of her theories will be correct. Quite simply, it's something real crazy going on with James, something he is manically worried about.

But Samasi, being a woman, will automatically internalize it and think it's her. She'll start sewing more and shopping less--even though she already was one for only buying things on sale, she'll purchase sex games from a friend of hers who sales sex toys, she'll start getting her hair done every week instead of every other week, she'll start looking thru James's stuff for new, odd numbers, visiting him at work unannounced with homemade lunches. She'll try all of that before flat-out asking him why he comes home so late and goes straight to bed without eating dinner lately, why he doesn't invite her out with the crew on Fridays anymore, why he's drastically cut down her spending money when the bills aren't any worse than they were before—only twenty dollars a week—that's what he gives her outside of money to pay the bills now! She'll wonder why he's always, *always* drunk on Saturday mornings nowadays, why he told her since she's always home *she* should rake the leaves, why he says "NO!" real loud and clear nowadays when she snuggles on top of him in the middle of the night, why he barely has more than two words to say to her after the little ones are off to sleep.

She will spend many a morning crying after he's left for work, on the phone with her grandma who was married to her granddad for sixty-five years before he passed and her grandma will only even more despairingly warn her that whenever it's a husband issue, it' a side hussy issue, and she will talk to her mother because her father—who thinks his Massie should still be a lover of Cabbage Patch dolls--will not care to listen to his babygirl sounding so hurt and he will pass the phone to her mom everyday around one o'clock in the afternoon and Samasi's mother will be so much more supportive and will tell her that maybe she should just give it time because James is a good man.

And it's not like she can call Nnevah about the situation. She and him haven't spoken since Cincinnati.

Add to this the fact that James is having a dinner party for The Drake and Chrissette's engagement and the whole situation becomes even more alarming--James talks to Chrissette on a regular basis *way more* than he talks to Samah these days.

It's month four of this shit and she's already feeling like a divorce is in order. Well, part of her. The other three/fourths of her knows this marriage is worth fighting for.

It's Chrissette and The Drake's engagement night. Everyone is there and, for the first within the last five months, James is acting normal towards Samasi. It's only the crew there and they've seen them argue before so it's not like he has to front for them. And it means so much to Samah that she takes James by the hand upstairs and gets some right after they serve dinner. But Nnevah is still acting weird and doesn't even say hello to Samah when he and Justina arrive. Nnevah and Justina seem to have swapped situations with James and Samah and seem to actually be doing quite well together these days. Nnevah sits on the same side of the table as Samah and James but down on the other end, which is kind of far since the middle, additional part of the dining table has been added. You can't even hear anyone asks for the hot sauce or the plate of lobster tails from that end. Plus, the music is blasting—some new electronica from Tokyo that Samasi is dying to ask Nnevah about but won't.

"I can't take this!" Samah, emotionally starved, will scream, month seven. The situation with James is still just as messed up. She's two seconds away from going ballistic and she can't stop screaming and she can't decide which is worse, the crying or the screaming. It would be nice to have adult conversation, a hug from the man the who signed the papers to be her husband—something! But, outside of Chrissette and The Drakes's engagement party, James has remained unchanged. Stone. Nothing nice. Grousing. Fault-finding. Nit-picking—like two days ago when he yelled at her for mopping the floor with the Swifter Mop instead of on her hands and knees like his mother's always done—which is why his mother's floors are so clean and why he doesn't mind when Baye tries to eat food off his mother's floor. But he can't even let Baye eat a piece of popcorn off *their* kitchen floor because she is too lazy and mops with the Swifter thingy! Lazy-that's what she is! And he huffed off and came back drunk as hell and Samah found the thirty-dollar receipt plus a ten-dollar tip from O' Grady's pub—that spot downtown cattycorner from Fishbones.

Her chest beats fast all day now. She can't take this. She can't even think. She wants to follow him but can't. She doesn't know what she will do if she sees the other woman.

When James comes home, he's in for a shocker. "What? Naw, you not going no where!"

"WATCH ME!" she screams like a victim of torture, packing the car with whatever she can see thru the tears. "YOU DON'T TALK TO ME, YOU DON'T SAY SHIT TO ME! YOU—YOU'RE ALWAYS GONE! I HATE YOU!!! FUCK THIS SHIT!!! THIS AIN'T LOVE—YOU DON'T LOVE ME!!!"

Maybe there can be some sort of saving, if he holds her real strong like he's done all the other times up until now, if he simply just takes her hand even and looks her really deeply in the eyes and says, "I love you, baby" like he's usually done up until now, even if he just says, "I know I been an ass-hole for the last seven months," that will work, too. And a simple "Here's why…" on top of that will only made her stay and wait even longer for him to act right. But he doesn't say any of it. And for some reason, even though he wants to, instead of saying or doing one of the right things a husband who has gotten himself in such a situation needs to say, he does the exact worst thing a husband in his situation can do. He opens his mouth-- giving her a few bouts of hope only to say, "Well, the kids aren't going. You can do whatever tha fuck you wanna do but my children aren't going anywhere. *Fuck you, bitch*!"

And for this reason, she does not doubt his love for her has long since ended.

When she reaches for Baye, he pushes her arm away and almost slams the door on her it.

James lets her take the newer car but not the kids.

Grandma Wilson opens the door and hugs Samasi warm and tender. Although Samasi knows only tender memories of Granny Wilson's house that smells like Pine-Sol mixed with old lady perfume and pig's feet and mustard greens and this will be home for as long as she needs it to be and although she now has the second bedroom to the left across from the bathroom with the leaky toilet and Grandma Wilson never bothers her when she doesn't feel like being bothered, Samasi still hates being there instead of at her own home and wonders what she did so terribly wrong to make James act like this. He's even changed the locks.

"Where you been?" It's Nnevah. Samasi is thinking it could be a set up but she is so desperate for conversation with someone other than her Grandmother and mother and, in desperation for information as to what's going on with James, she talks anyway.

"What do you mean where have *I* been! James is acting crazy—for the last seven months he's been acting different! I left! And he won't let me see the kids or keep them! And I don't even understand what's going on."

"WHAT? You serious?"

"Yeah."

"Where are you?"

She sighs. "My grandmother's"

"Where? I'm about to come over."

"Off Rosa Park and the Boulevard. On Blaine. 4590 Blaine."

"Gimme a few minutes to wrap some shit up I got going on over here. I'll be there in a lil bit."

Thirty minutes later Nnevah calls Samah back. "Yeah, I'm out here. I don't know how ya grandma is so I didn't wanna come to the door."

Samah's not thinking she shouldn't trust Nnevah or that this could be something ill and is sitting on the passenger side of his truck within seconds.

"What tha fuck? You serious? That nigga hasn't said shit about this to any of us. You sure you two aren't just having one of your regular things that'll be over next week or some shit?"

"Nnevah. Something's *wrong*. We haven't even had sex since Chrissette and The Drake's engagement party. And before that? It was like—like at the Cincinnati Jazz Festival and that's it. Something's wrong. My grandma thinks he's cheating. I don't know. When you don't know you start thinking all kinda stuff. I don't think he would cheat but…I don't—I don't know—I don't know what I've done to him to make him hate me."

Nnevah sighs. "Man, I'm just gon' tell you." And before Samasi's heart has a chance to bristle up in preparation for all the answers she really may not want to know, Nnevah turns and says to her, "Man, Samasi, fuck that bitch ass nigga. I've known him since fourth grade and he's lucky as hell to have a woman like you. He hasn't said shit to me—whatever it is, he already knows I'ma be on your side. You need to fuck tha dumb shit and let that nigga go. He doesn't know how to handle you. He got's that short man's complex and shit...

"Lobster and spam don't belong on the same dining room table..." and before he says anything else Samah laughs.

Samah does not know that Nnevah had peeped them fucking that day at the engagement party. He'd gone upstairs to use the bathroom and witnessed all six minutes of it thru the bedroom door that was cracked open. And he had stayed in the bathroom jacking off and shit thinking about it—minus the James part--and fighting the urge to come on to Samasi that night by staying the fuck away from her fine ass.

"I hate to see you going thru *any* of this. I'll look out for you." And, for some reason, Samasi believes he will.

"Matter fact, why don't you go get dressed, we'll go grab something to eat." Nnevah knows not to go in too hard for the kill. It won't work with her type. A woman like Samasi is too loyal to give up on James just yet. Then, too, it'll make her not want to be with him; she won't feel like she'll be able to trust him. Nnevah is a little hood, has a masters in marketing, bachelors in business, is a very well-read young man and has been checking Samasi out since James had started bringing her around back in the day. He knows her backwards and forward, their friendship only solidifying his inklings on Samasi's inner workings and mindset. But, really, he doesn't even need all that. Nnevah knows he's a looker. And he knows timing is everything--specifically why he's here right now. Couldn't be better timing—especially when he and Justina just called everything off last night. All she was was a good blow job any fucking way--the kind of bitch that didn't do shit but lay there in missionary when they fucked and kept admonishing him not to mess up her hair… Sometimes a man needs something that can do more than just breathe and look good at his parties.

    Samasi comes out looking nice, casual outfit and all. Nnevah asks her if she wants to go to 2941 but Samasi knows James frequents the spot. Instead they go to Bahama Breeze not too far from Somerset, spend only a little time on what Nnevah considers a trifle dubbed James and they spend most of the evening catching back up on the music thing they had going on—four new artists; one from Paris, one from Cairo and two straight from the D.

    Of course, that night he knew he wasn't going to get it, but he was now more than half way close to getting her.

    This will continue. Just like James not letting her see the kids will continue. And, seamlessly, Massie will be hanging out with Vah just for diversion's sake and Vah'll prove to be the perfect escape to the loneliness and the reverberating emptiness dwelling inside her. Nnevah's the perfect everything and her grandmother will tell her that she understands and that she's got the right to move forward with her life and shortly after that she'll stop leaving Nnevah's crib at night.

Massie thinks about going back to social work like she was doing before she had Baye but, after Vah takes her to a knitting and crocheting trade show, she decides to start her own knitting thing instead which begins to create a nice buzz around town. On the weekends she helps Vah out with his gigs and unintentionally impress a few people Nnevah has contracts with which helps him get even more gigs—gigs out of the country. Lucky him.

Things go so well for them that, the only way they even remember life without being together every night is because of the custody issue.

Samasi has already filed for divorce. Next month, July seventh she will face James in court. Til then, the daily, early morning drive by's when she watches James lug the kids to the garage and the evening drive by's at six when she watches James carry the kids in the house with him will have to suffice. Whenever she calls and asks to see the kids James says, "NO—HOE!" Then hangs up on her.

"Your honor, I ask that the court give me blah, blah, blah, blah, blah…" All the things Samasi does not want to hear. James has shown up today without a lawyer--a ploy Vah prepared her for—especially now that James knows they live together. Vah says James will try to do whatever he can to stall. He's heard from The Drake and Chrissette that James wants her back. Badly. James is now depressed. He is now tired of playing Mr. Mom. His mother is always traveling and just doesn't have the time to raise another set of kids--

his kids--cause hers are all grown! Watching her son's kids—while "their nasty mother is out shacking up with her baby's childhood friend! What a shame! What a down right nasty shame! No wonder the Black race was so lost these days—these young girls don't know how to do anything except skeeze on these poor young men. And to think at one time she actually liked Samasi! The skank!" Mother Meyers knew one thing for sure: the bible said for better or worse and that Samasi skank wasn't living up to her end of the bargain; Samasi was hurting her son, James. Even if they had problems, Samasi was wrong for leaving James!

But Samasi is at the point where she is over it. Now, almost a year later—because he had started pulling this mess way back in August—now James wanted to come around!

Life doesn't work that way. Samasi was going to be the one to show him!

They leave with a court issued order for counseling. Not a good look. Had she known it was going to turn out like this, she *would have* let Vah come to court like he wanted. She thought it'd be too much. All that face-to-face crap. Already James was staring her down with the most pitiful look taking over his entire face.

God what had she seen in him. He was *nice*—well, *was* nice at one time. But that was all he had had going for him. He wasn't half as sexy as Vah. She must have been closing her eyes during that James shit.

It's amazing how your perception of people can change right before your very eyes for better or worse, all because of their inner qualities and the way they behave.

When Vah finds out, he is not at all happy about it. He hadn't thought about the judge ordering counseling—it wasn't like you could force someone to stay with you. James was finally trying to grow some balls all of a sudden, aye?

Nnevah knows he is the one for Samasi. Best man at the wedding, best man still…

Nnevah thinks he's got it all down to a science.

But things don't go like that in love. Samasi *is* strongly in love with Vah—can't get that fact twisted--however, secretly, secretly Samassi is wondering and has always wondered since this affair began, if Nnevah just has some kind of vendetta against James—if he is just doing all this as some sort of payback. She wonders if maybe something happened recently with the two and Vah is on the revenge tip.

"Okay. Glad you both made it," the counselor, a Caucasian lady of about sixty begins once Samasi sits on the other couch cattycorner to the one James is sitting on with his legs crossed. Samasi has arrived slightly later than five-thirty to avoid being in the waiting room with James. "I'd like to start out by talking to you both separately. Who would like to go first?"

Samasi does not move. Does not budge. Arms folded, lips and fingers tense and a foot that will not stop tapping the carpet.

James, who cannot bear to look her way, reaches an arm on the back of the couch and swallows so loud the two of them hear it.

"James, would you like to start?" The counselor asks.

He does not reply although this whole thing is his wish now granted.

"Okay then, James, we'll start with you--" and before the counselor has a chance to say anything else, Samasi is already taking a seat in the hallway.

Samasi's plan? To say nothing except, "I want joint custody of my babies" and "he refuses to let me see them," which would have worked except the counselor was on some nouveaux bull.

"Write down all the things that first attracted you to James, Samasi. I'll give you five minutes," which was so unnecessary; the heart with the dagger in it took less than thirty seconds for Samasi to draw. "Okay. Next, I'd like you to write down all the things you are currently not happy with within the relationship." The counselor lady says totally seeing but ignoring the huge heart/dagger thing.

For this second request, Samasi draws a frowning face. Only because she wants her kids.

"Now. Breathe."

What? This wasn't yoga. Instead, Samasi stares her deadpan in the face.

"...Okay. Now, I'd like you to write down all the things you'd like to see materialize within your relationship with James."

Samasi scribbles Taemar and Baye in huge, fancy, cursive letters.

"Okay... Now. I'd like to look over your worksheets." She glances over Samasi's paper and compares it with James', which from the back, looks like a lot of essay paragraphs. "Your sheet says a lot, Samasi. Over the next few weeks, I'd really like to help repair your relationship with James. James wants to save the marriage... How do you feel about that?"

"I want joint custody of my kids."

"Okay... And how do you feel about saving your marriage."

"He refuses to let me see them."

The counselor lady will try one more time to see that it will only happen again. She dismisses Samasi and retains James.

"How do you currently feel?" the counselor asks James who is preoccupied with staring at the dent on the side of her desk. He wonders who did it; if maybe it was Samasi. It looks like a fresh dent. If Samasi *did* do it, then that's good. Maybe it shows that she still cares. People do stuff like that when their emotions are strong. You can't be mad if you don't care, right? Or maybe that's not it at all. Maybe Samasi kicked her desk because the court ordered her to come and she's pissed she's not in the bed fucking that Judas Nnevah right now! Et tu Brutes! And why does he even still want that bitch when she's shown her ass, anyway? Fuckin' ass cunt! Prostitute! He says the word to himself three more times and when he's done, when he doesn't feel like thinking the word again, he still wishes she was holding his hand right now. He'd still give his life for her. "...How do you currently feel?" The counselor inquires.

James, who'd rather say *I want my wife at home, she's supposed to be that bitch--no matter what goes down, she's supposed to be there--she's supposed to have my back. I know I was ill but I love that girl—she should know that—look at all that time I spent chasin' after her when she wasn't feelin' me. I never cheated on her—wouldn't ever cheat on her... How could she just walk off like this? She doesn't know what I've been going thru...*

Instead of saying anything, he simply shrugs a few seconds before quietly stating, "I love my wife." And leaves it at that.

In the car, James sits silently for the next hour while running his thumb across his wedding band. The wedding band. He's never, ever taken it off. He rewinds Samasi's face when she came in to the counseling session... The way she's dressing slightly different now—more fancy... The way her hairstyle is totally new and the fact that she was wearing a new perfume and not wearing her wedding ring. Then, James' chest gets tight—like when you have a good case of the Flu. He starts thinking about how his boss came on to him that Monday right after they got back from Cincinnati and how Jim that faggot assed Vice President and his boss had came to the office late that evening he stayed to finish his report and how they both had dragged him into the stock room and unzipped his pants and smacked him when he said no and how they'd tried to tie him up but how he'd punched Jim and how nothing has felt the same since that day even though they both transferred the next week. How could he go to human resources with a thing like that?

Samasi is understanding. This James knows. But he does not want her to know about the situation. He made a promise to protect her the day they got married and he was going to keep that promise. Samasi would be worried about him, asking him questions he didn't want her asking. And maybe she would think he had done something with them before or maybe she would think they'd forced themselves on him and that he was lying to cover the rest of the story up. And his new bonus—she'd think that was because he had given in...

But he had never been down with that type of shit and *wasn't ever* going to be!

James' phone rings. It's his mother. She's probably ready for him to get the kids. Lately, now that she's not as messed up over his dad's slow, cancer-induced death, she's been dating dudes with thick, white beards who like to go to MGM to gamble and eat and wear loafers with pennies stuck in them. James is certain he doesn't like this but right now that was the least of his concerns. Besides, his mother seems a lot happier these days than she ever did with his father—the cheating, lying bastard. James had said he'd never be like James Senior. And he wasn't. But this shit was just as bad. Losing his wife over a sick and twisted situation. Whenever he closes his eyes, those two guys are there, Jim Guys and Gary Nixon, shoving him into the stock room...

Then there are the questions. Like *why* did they pick him? Did he *look* like he was gay or some shit? Was it because he was short? It seemed like dudes always tried to test him because he was short.

He ignores his mother's missed call alerts and goes to the bar across the street. The next day he calls off work when he wakes up and finds himself in the counselor's parking lot, in the car at 8:55 in the morning.

"How did it go?" Vah asks Samasi the minute she walks in the door and drops her purse on the marble countertop. Normally, on Wednesdays he goes to The Illingsworth Club across the street from Campus Martius downtown and hangs out for a while with the owners. Back in the day they used to all go over to the Canadian strip clubs after they closed up The Illingsworth for the night. But these days, with Samasi around, he's been doing a few weekday cameo appearances with Samasi at his side at the clubs and coming straight home on the nights she didn't feel like rolling with him.

Samasi is different like that. She doesn't bother him about hanging out or his job. She knows it's what he does. Justina—with all her yelling and popping up and shit--wasn't *anything* like that. Justina was forever swearing he was cheating. Justina's number one suspect? Samasi. Justina was forever bringing it up.

Then again, what if Samasi wasn't tripping on him because...because *she* was still hooking up with *James*? And then there was Yusef, that one promoter he was working with on the new Arista Project... Yusef had made a couple comments about how fine Samasi was and he had given him an increased percentage on the next couple of gigs they would be working on...

All women got jealous. No woman Nnevah had ever dated was cool with his schedule or how the ladies were sometimes on him at club events—which, he had toned down since he'd gotten with Samasi. Something had to be up with her, though. *Was* something up with her? Or maybe she was just *that* cool, right? ...No.

What if she didn't care about him the same way she cared about James? What if she was just trying to piss James off and she and James were about to work their problems out and he was going to be the one to wind up hurt in the long run?

These questions go thru Nnevah's head all the time. But for some reason--for lots of reasons, Nnevah loves this girl and he doesn't want to let her go.

Tonight he's going to have to put it on her—to make her forget all about James. Or Yusef? He's gonna have to figure out a way to get her to get out of this court ordered shit. And that's not going to be easy with kids involved. Already Vah has thrown out five of her birth control pills one by one.

"It sucked. And I *don't* wanna talk about it. All I want is joint custody of the kids. I've got to get the lawyer to get this counseling shit 86-ed."

Yeah, we've always been on the same page Ma, Nnevah thinks to himself. Good. But if it's not James, is it Yusef, then?

"Nnevah?"

"What, baby?"

"I love you. I'm sorry all of this craziness is going on."

Nnevah leans down and kisses all the lipgloss off Samasi's lips. He pulls out that long, thick dick of his and gives it to her right there on the counter. The way he sucks the arched line right in the middle of her feet and the way he rolls his tongue around each and every one of her toes while he is still deep inside her makes Massie shake and shake and squirt and shake. She's never squirted before Nnevah.

He's still rock hard and the sounds she makes make precum drip off the tip of his dick. She can barely slide him all the way between her big toe and second toe but gives him a foot job before they go in the bedroom and make love. There is a shadow against the bedroom wall of two lust-filled seesaws pushing each other to further and further heights.

"Thanks for coming, Samasi," the counselor states rather monotonously as Samasi steps in twenty minutes late, morose since her lawyer has just informed her that she must attend these shits for the sake of the custody battle that, from the looks of it, is going to become the battle from Hades.

James sighs a sigh that Samasi will take as ass-hole-ness but is really of relief. He had been thinking that maybe she was seriously done and just going to walk out on the children. The children. All the bitch seems to care about when she calls. She doesn't say "Hi," she doesn't ask, "How are you?" All she asks about is the children. So be it. They're his, too. And she's not getting them. Not unless she brings her ass back to where she had no business leaving in the first muthafuckin' place!

On this day, they are both so tuned out to the rest of the world and, even more so tuned out to each other, nothing the counselor says will be heard. For the remaining thirty-nine minutes to both of them the counselor sounds like dead air, like when the television station used to go off at night back in the day.

James hangs around in the waiting room since Samasi left out five minutes before the session was supposed to end with some stupid excuse. He thinks she is probably hiding out in the restroom near the elevator waiting for him to leave the parking lot.

He is correct. Samasi is sitting on the couch in the lounge area of the restroom flipping thru a knitting magazine enduring the foul air some lady in the handicapped stall is creating.

James finally leaves thinking he just doesn't know Samasi anymore.

She waits four minutes later before heading to the elevator only to bump into the counselor in the parking lot. "Samasi?"

Samasi pretends not to hear her but quickly changes her mind since the counselor has the power to make her look bad to the court.

"Samasi? ...James really does love you, dear. I think you two need to talk. Soon... I'd like you to try something... It would be very helpful if you wrote down what it is you feel James has done that has hurt you. Write it out and, either give it to him or throw it away, the choice is yours. But I can tell you two love each other deeply. You two have the power to create a new beginning."

Samasi gives the counselor a starchy smile and drives off. She drives and drives before she realizes that she's almost at James's house. She parks a block over and is just in time to see his mother carrying Baye into the house. Where is Taemar? Must already be inside--the door is open. James' mother doesn't go inside. It looks like his mother is shaking her head or something but Samasi cannot tell what else is going from where's she's parked.

Inside, after he shuts off the "skanky wife" remarks his mother doles out right in front of his children's ears, he shuts the door and puts the kids to bed early thinking about how Samasi is missing out on Baye's new tooth that's coming in. He thinks about taking a picture and texting it to her then curses at himself for even thinking of doing such a thing. If the bitch wants to be around her kids, she knows what she's going to have to do: come home! That's how he feels.

He's so angry he can't read to Taemar tonight. He can't sleep in the bed either. He has one of Samasi's shirts laid out on the side of the bed she used to sleep in.

Hennessey is all he's going to do for the rest of the night.

He's going have to be hard on Samasi in order to get her to stop doing him so bogus; it's just like when you bump your knee and have to apply pressure on it to make the pain stop.

Nnevah is thinking Samasi should have been home by now. He was waiting on her to come for dinner. It's sweet how she fixed it for him and had his plate saran wrapped in the refrigerator. He wants to chill with her tonight. He's going out in an hour and hopes she'll ride with him.

"Hey, Nnevah."

Subconsciously it bothers him that she hasn't been calling him Vah lately.

"Hey. Where you been?"

She doesn't respond.

"I godda make a run tonight, you feel like rolling with me?"

"Where?"

"Baker's Keyboard Lounge."

"Yeah, did you eat yet?"

"Naw, I was waiting for you."

"*Awww*, ba*aabb*y!"

That's even better than her calling him Vah. The way she says anything always sounds so sincere.

During and after dinner everything is perfect until they step into Bakers. The Drake, who has been able to manage still being okay with Nnevah up until now, is there. Seeing Nnevah with Samasi? That shit makes him feel like it's straight up ill.

He walks up to the couple and says, "Y'all ain't right… Y'all ain't right," rubs his goatee and calls James-- James who is too drunk at this point and fast asleep on the living room floor with Harold Melvin and The Bluenotes "I Miss You" playing.

"Man, I ain't got shit to prove to you," Nnevah responds still holding Samasi's hand, passing up The Drake and walking over to some other fellas he knows.

"Baby, you know we gonna get that? We're gonna run into them and we're gonna get that. But I love you. And I don't give a fuck what none of these muthafuckas out here got to say. They don't know the situation," Vah says later that night once they are in bed. He is holding Massie just the way she likes to be held, not too tight and very gently.

"Baby, I know. People are always gonna have something to say. But they weren't there when I was begging James to love me and shit. He's turned into the type of guy who's gotten comfortable and doesn't wanna do the work it takes to keep a relationship going. He's becoming just like how he said his father was—that type that thinks a woman's place is to suffer in silence and to deal with whatever bullshit a man puts on her. James, The Drake, they can feel *however* they want to feel but I'm not about to be stuck in a loveless marriage. It's like I'm supposed to be a trophy he can leave sitting on the mantle while he goes off and lives and I only get attention when he feels like picking me up and dusting me off for a second. I already went thru that with my first husband. The thing that gets me is that he *knew all this*. He knew I wasn't going to deal with another situation like that all over again. Why did he even marry me if he wasn't going to do anything but act like this! Vah? I'm sorry. I hate to discuss this mess with you."

"Naw, baby, you godda get that shit off your chest." Actually, he's relieved she's speaking on it. She'd been real quiet lately.

"...Vah?" the way she says his name, long and sweet like a saccharine song, as hard and masculine as he is, it still drives him crazy. He can remember the first time they met the way she'd said it just like that.

"...I love you..." Samasi adds.

Nnevah responds with gentle fingertips on her bare arms.

Instead of saying anything else, the two linger between the sheets with the window slightly cracked, the wind and the midtown traffic seeping thru and they listen to some of their favorite records on the old school stereo as the music plays in the living room and drifts into their bedroom.

This time, in court today, things will be drastically different. Judge Ryson, who has normally been fair and business-like changes her complete demeanor when Samasi walks in stomach poking out, maternity shirt and all.

"You mean to tell me you haven't seen your kids, you quit going to counseling and *you're pregnant*, Mrs. Meyers?"

Since Samasi hasn't budged, James has started this whole unfit to be a mother thing.

But this? This seeing Samasi looking like she's got a pillow tucked under her shirt? This pushes him over the edge!

"Mr. Meyers, are you sure you would like to continue to sue the plantiff for an appeal? After deliberation it is—"

"--Your Honor, I *want my* marriage! I'm willing let her have visitation rights, Your Honor. I want to make our marriage work."

"Mr. Meyers the plaintiff—"

"--Your Honor! If my wife wants to end the counseling sessions, that's fine. If she'll agree to—"

"--Your Honor," Samasi interrupts. "This man right here," she raises her eyebrows and points her thumb in James's direction, "is only doing this out of spite. I would like to go thru with the divorce. *All this time* he's never said

I could see the kids until now! You weren't there when I was trying to get this man to talk to me and he wouldn't say anything to me for over seven months! *He* chose not to let me see the kids—"

"--Mrs. Meyers, *YOU* COULD HAVE GONE TO SEE YOUR KIDS! *YOU'RE* THEIR MOTHER! YOU THINK SOMEBODY COULD HOLD ME BACK FROM MY CHILDREN—AND YOU GOT BABIES MRS. MEYERS! YOU WALKED OFF AND LEFT BABIES! YOUR HUSBAND WAS TAKING CARE OF YOU AND YOU WALKED OFF—YOU MUST NOT HAVE UNDERSTOOD YOUR VOWS—FOR *BETTER OR WORSE*! THEY ARE RAMIFICATIONS FOR BAD DECISIONS MRS. MEYERS! I SEE HERE THAT THIS IS YOUR SECOND MARRIAGE? DID YOU GET UPSET AND WALK OFF THE FIRST TIME, TOO?"

"Your Honor, with all respect, you don't know me! You didn't live in my house with my first husband and you aren't the one married to James, either—"

"--MRS. MEY-YERS! YOU HAVE A *HUSBAND* WHO LOVES YOU AND WANTS TO LOVE YOU BUT, FOR WHATEVER REASON, HAD SOME THINGS HE NEEDED TO WORK ON! THIS MAN WANTS YOU—EVEN THOUGH *YOU ARE OBVIOUSLY* CARRYING ANOTHER MAN'S CHILD! DO YOU UNDERSTAND WHAT IS GOING ON HERE?

"IT LOOKS LIKE YOU'RE COMING UP WITH EXCUSES TO MAKE YOUR ADULTEROUS NEW RELATIONSHIP SEEM OKAY!

"Mr. Meyers, was she married to her previous husband when you two started dating?"

"No, ma'am. And Your Honor, I'd like to say something. I know I did some things that might have pushed my wife away, but I love her and I know she loves me. She's living with a guy I grew up with! I believe he's the one that talked her into leaving! I know him and I know he's the type that likes to play mind games and--"

"—NO! NO! MIND GAMES? IF ANYBODY'S PLAYING ANYTHING—ESPECIALLY THIS NEW LIL VICTIM ROLE, IT'S *YOU*, JAMES!" Samasi spazzes out. She's so pissed, her veins pop out of her neck.

"Mrs. Meyers, the manner in which you're defending this guy you're having an affair with—this suddenly defensive demeanor of yours—I'm wondering if, in fact, Mr. Meyers--"

Samasi has lost her cool. She huffs and puffs and shakes her hands in the air and tries to hold back all the things running thru her head. She laughs sarcastically. "Your Honor? If I was *a man*, you'd grant the divorce and it wouldn't even be a big deal. If I was a man who had left his kids with his wife, nothing about this--*none* of this would be a big deal. You'd probably tell James that he couldn't be with someone that didn't want to be with him and that, eventually, he'd move on. Problem is, I didn't just walk off. I *still don't know* to this day if James was cheating all those months he was coming home late and pushing me off him every night. *This man right* here cut up all my clothes and dumped them outside one time when I tried to visit the kids—and I'm over it. You don't see me in here asking about money for a new wardrobe or asking for half of what he's got or alimony or anything other than joint custody of my children. I'm *done* with the entire situation with the exception of getting along for the sake of our kids. I don't have to stay married to someone, who, until a few minutes ago wasn't acting like he cared if I was still alive or dead." She folds her hands across her chest and twists her neck at the judge.

"...Your Honor, I know I wasn't a hundred percent there for Samasi last year but I've been there all the other times."

"James? You're doing this out of spite and you—"

"--ORDER IN THE COURT! ORDER, MRS. MEYERS! THE COURT IS TAKING A TEN-MINUTE RECESS!"

During this break, Samasi turns to face James for the first time. He looks back at her and she notices the tear. There is no one else save the lawyers in the courtroom.

"Samah..." That is all James says. And it is enough. Right then at that moment, she understands how much he really does love her.

She opens her mouth to ask why he hasn't tried until now but cannot say anything. She simply swallows hard and clutches the podium she is standing behind.

Then there is Nnevah. Who she loves and in three more months will be having a child with.

Some cannot get love. Rarely do we have too much or an abundance of love.

When the judge comes back and takes a seat, she looks down on Samasi from her bench and says after a long, hard breath/groan. "The court rules in favor of the defendant, James Meyers." She bangs her gavel. "Mrs. Meyers, I'm giving you a chance to think," she adds.

And that is it, the decision that will help make things all the more harder.

When Samasi walks out of the courtroom, she won't notice that James is right behind her until he touches her finger. She'd know his touch if she was dead.

"Can we go somewhere and talk?" he asks doing well not to stare at her round belly.

Samah nods yes. Both of them have parked at the casino because it was cheaper. James gets in his car and follows her car to Anita's Kitchen in Ferndale--James' suggestion.

They both instantly remember the way Baye was laughing at James' comments about his mother and his aunt. James and Samasi act like things are as good as that one day of the Ferndale Festival.

Nnevah is texting and texting Samah **WHERE THA HELL R U????** just like Justina used to text him. And Samah is ignoring him like he used to ignore Justina.

They sit across from one another in the booth, looking away and looking at each other at the same times.

"I'm sorry, Samah. Sorry for everything. I messed up, Samah. I know. But I really want us to work. I wanna make sure we work out."

Samah is starting to realize just how easy it is to mess up. And that everyone does at some time or another. Imperfection's killer con.

So where do we go from here? They both want to ask but don't.

"Let's work it out," James says. His voice is as soothing as it used to be.

"…I don't know what we're gonna do," she responds. He walks her to her car. They don't hug. He just opens the car door for her and watches her drive down Woodward.

When Samasi comes home to Nnevah, he is on the phone and shuts his office door. A few minutes later he goes into the kitchen where Samasi is washing her hands at the sink.

"You ain't get none of my texts?" He is using anger to disguise the possibility of a bad court-hearing decision.

"Yeah…" She knows he's worried and excuses his attitude.

"…I got some good news," he announces a little later, turning to her and hugging her.

"Yeah?"

"…We're moving to Miami…"

Samasi is immediately thinking Nnevah is doing this because of this whole mess and that *is* partly it but Nnevah is doing a lot more work down there lately and it would be a smart move. It's a move he's been plotting on longer than Samasi.

"Two weeks from now--I already got a spot down there. 'Member that time we all went last year and stayed at The Grand? *That* place. My boy is renting it out to us."

Samasi pulls away from him. "Nnevah…baby, look. The judge ruled against me—I'm still not divorced from James. And—and then there's the kids. Which, *now* James is saying I can see them. I can't *move* to Florida, baby."

But when the day arrives and the movers come, Massie will be on the plane with Nnevah.

Samasi starts crocheting outfits for this singer who just signed onto the biggest label in New York and she gets even more connections thru Vah's connections. Her business starts going so well she ends up renting a store not too far from the Miami Tribune.

They become even closer because Vah does things like take her for strolls early in the morning along the South Beach shore and things like surprising Massie with flowers even when it's not Valentine's Day or her birthday and they never really argue like she and James sometimes did. None of it is because Nnevah is plotting. It's all strictly out of love.

Massie has a girl who looks just like Nnevah and Nnevah wakes up in the middle of the night right along with Massie when the baby fusses—even after he comes in at three in the morning from an event.

But James keeps calling and Samasi sneaks and talks to him when Nnevah is fast asleep or out at gigs.

James never stops telling her he loves her.

When Samasi comes to Michigan on business with Vah and to visit the kids, she spends the night at James' house. Although Vah wants to, he doesn't ask too much about it. She always says they just talked, which is true. But eventually that changes.

Nnevah always drives her over to James' whenever they go to Michigan and picks her up the next morning. Then they get on the plane and go back to Miami.

When Nnevah proposes to her, Massie says "yes" and their two daughters stand in the wedding not technically considered 'legal,' but still legal in his heart and in her heart and to everyone knowing them. Vah and Massie become husband and wife.

One day when Taemar and Baye and Alyse and Ayana get older they will wonder why mommy travels so much and sometimes is gone the entire month.

One day, years and years later, when you have completely forgotten about this story, there will be a big, big funeral—the kind everyone talks about even years later.

There will be a ninety-six year old lady with two bands on her ring finger, a platinum band and a yellow gold band. And there will be all these grand kids and great-grand kids... And three daughters who look oddly similar to each other even though one is brown and two are of carmel complexion. When Taemar and Baye and Alyse and Ayana find out, as they bury their mother in Michigan between Nnevah Taylor and James Meyers, they will all initially be infuriated with their mother, Samah Meyers/Massie Taylor. They'll be so pissed their fathers took that shit from their mother. James never brought other women home and was faithful to their mother. Nnevah could have cheated with all the swarms of women buzzing around him even after he sold his nightclubs and bars but he never did anything with any of them. As an old man Nnevha had aged pretty well and could have kept much younger ladies around on the side but was just never interested.

Sixty and fifty somethings act like kids when it comes to sibling rivalry issues and feuds.

Taemar clearly remembers when Baye cheated on that one girl he'd been with for three years in college. James had gone off on him, "Black men need to stop trying to be players and pimps—if you got a bad one, dump her and if you have a good one, you need to be on top of ya game, man!" Dad had truly been in love with their mother, always talking about her and telling them not to be mad when she couldn't make it to flute recitals and basketball games—"she is working hard and really loves you two," he'd say. Their poor dad.

And Alyse and Ayana will wonder how come their mom just didn't divorce that James guy or why their father hadn't dated anyone when she was "out of town." Alyse will be so upset, she'll want to pull her mother out of her grave to curse her mother out—especially for all the times she had to be pulled out of school to travel abroad with dad—he was probably just lonely—that's probably the only reason he had made her go with him—dad had said it was because she "was getting too bored with school and slipping on grades" but Alyse was almost certain the only reason he'd made her go with him was because he was lonely—he never had chicks around except ma! Alyse had to be tutored while she was out of town missing school and always ended up being called into the kitchen almost every time they went out to eat because dad would brag to restaurant owners about how "she could throw down in a kitchen" or he'd ask the restaurant owners to teach her how to make something off their menu and later dad would have her show mom--mom who was too busy *flu-flu-flussying* around "out of town." It would have been nice to go out to dinner for once without having to help fix the food! Alyse will think back to that one time in Japan when she was fourteen when dad was on that techno festival committee and she taught chef Miyo her mom's famous fried chicken recipe in exchange for his eight layered sushi roll secret she still will not share to this day with her kitchen staff. She laughs in retrospect. Especially at how dad would keep an eye on her and scared all the boys off which, wasn't funny back then. Then, Alyse will think about how her mother had sent grocery lists and cooking directions by email and would coach her thru dinner over the phone and how she'd landed that internship at NBC's Rainbow Room way back in the day all because she'd become an excellent cook who'd always had to fill-in in the kitchen when her mother was "gone on business."

And Ayana will be tied between hating her deceased mother for making her go straight to the store after school and she'd have to do her homework first then help in the front of the store. Because of that she had no life and missed out on being a normal teenaged girl who could hang out at the mall with her friends or take up after school activities. Ayana will be pissed about all those hours she had to put in at the store in the summer because they were always backed up on pieces and mom was sometimes gone, "taking care of business." A lot of the times when dad and Alyse were out of town, she and her mother had to stay behind in Miami because of the boutique. They would spend the night in the boutique and only go home to shower or to fix something to eat. It always pissed Ayana that she couldn't go out of town with Alyse and her father. This time in her fifties, the memory will anger Ayana but not completely. Part of her will be glad she was at the store so much—that was how she'd met legend LG the rapper's son—her music producer husband of thirty some odd years now. And being at that shop all the time was how she'd become well connected with quite a few kid's of celebrities who were always there with their mothers shopping at her mother's knitting boutique. Ayana will remember how the store was like a second home and how her dad would always come there before he'd do a late night event and how he'd sometimes take a nap in the back on the futon and make mom come with him—"she needs to rest sometimes," he'd say and Ayana would have to turn up the surround sound to block out all the noises her parents were making on the futon...

And Taemar and Baye will refuse to acknowledge Alyse and Ayana. Baye will hate the fact that Alyse and Ayana are much taller than him—that maybe he could have been drafted in the NBA if he would have been as tall as them--how did Ayana have the nerve to be six-one? Baye will think about the time he told his father he wished his then wife now ex wasn't around so much to nag and complain all the damn time and will remember asking his dad how he and mom had managed to stay married so long and still be so in love. Baye had even told James he probably *would have* still been married to Makayla if they wouldn't have had to see each other's faces day in and day out. All James had said was, "Son, when it's love, you'll know it and you won't be able to do a damn thing about it..." and then James had chuckled.

Taemar and Baye, thinking about how their mother had put them on the back burner for no reason at all other than selfishness, will continue ignoring Alyse's and

Ayana's calls... All the times Samasi would say, "I'll be right back, sweetie" to Taemar as she grabbed her phone and went to the basement and stayed on the phone forever. All the times she had told Taemar, "A lot of other teenage girls have the same problems you have, sweetie. You're not the only one..." No wonder! All the more reason to ignore Alyse's and Ayana's calls! Those two women were relentless--they just kept calling and calling! Taemar and Baye will act just as stubborn as their father.

...Until one day when they vaguely begin to remember going to concerts in Miami and playing with these two girls and going out of town to Toronto and seeing them in a hotel lobby; that one year Baye became a permanent basketball addict and they had season box seats at the Little Caesars Arena and went to every game and sometimes two girls--who looked like they could have been Alyse and Ayana when they were kids—those two girls sometimes were seated next to them. Baye will recall liking one of those girls and how his mother screamed in horror when Taemar told her about Baye's secret crush.

Baye will also remember that day he almost totaled his father's car and how his mother was "out of town" and he called her at three in the morning and she had immediately picked up and listened without yelling and cursing him out like he thought she was going to do and he'll think about how she called his father and talked to James and sent him the money on Pay Pal three hours later to pay the collision shop. His father was going to make him work an after school job the rest of the year to pay it off but mom, she had talked dad out of it—"college was right around the corner," she'd said. "That boy needs to stay on the basket ball team and to keep those grades up so he can get scholarships, James."

And Taemar will be thinking and thinking about that time those Noleson twins were bullying her and had stolen her phone and, how she'd emailed her mother about it and her mom had called her a few minutes later and told her exactly what "to tell them lil bitches" which Tae had done and, because of that—standing up for herself without bringing her mama to school to have a meeting with Principal Dumar like all the other girls in her class had done, Taemar had ended up being the most popular girl in middle school there on out and everybody knew not to mess with her!

Taemar will initiate the phone call with Baye on three-way. They'll meet with Alyse and Ayana for a dinner that will began rather chilly but end with funny stories about that Mrs. Meyers/Taylor lady, who, until a year ago when Nnevah passed, knitted and sewed and crocheted all the time and was always sewing a great-grandbaby an outfit and could go so fast she'd finish a piece in one day…that old lady who, up until a few months ago when James passed, had still put on lipstick, cooked big, big meals and put on heels…

Christmases will be larger there on out, family portraits and pictures will be swapped and they will skip the "step" part when introducing each other to long time friends.

All said and done, Taemar, a retired music teacher who still teaches private piano lessons, Baye, a retired gym coach who volunteers at the Boys and Girls Club, Alyse, a world renown chief and Ayana, who'd taken her mother's knitting and sewing and crocheting to the runway and started her own fashion house and was now turning it over to her daughter—Samasi--named after her doting granny, they, Taemar and Baye will decide to stop resenting the lifestyle their mother had shared with Alyse and Ayana and Alyse and Ayana will decide to stop feeling like Taemar and Baye'd had a more normal family than what'd they'd had growing up. They'll decide they'd all had better childhoods than most of their peers and finally understand just how much their mother loved her family...

Adaptation

Daniel holds the door open for Theena as they enter Fitzgerald's the city's hottest new restaurant and bar in midtown. Another couple and security are with them. The minute they step in the place a few people flood over to their table—as husky as Daniel and his boy are, there's no way to miss them. Daniel and Zabar had a game in Detroit and brought the girls along. Security does a good job keeping the fans away without being rude—this is part of Daniel's and Zabar's contracted events. The restaurant's band isn't that great or that bad either but the small crowd doesn't seem to care. Theena is sitting next to Daniel who is kissing the temple of her forehead and whispering on and on about how sexy she looks tonight. The girls haven't been able to spend a night out with their guys in three weeks with all the games and appearances. Theena is more than happy to be getting some from Daniel tonight but not at all happy about being in this city. She secretly wishes to never come back. *Let the past stay in the past and don't look back like Lot's wife*, Theena thinks.

Just like Theena figures, a few minutes after they order appetizers here comes Daphnie, a bar hopping regular and a girl, until a few months ago, Theena had been kind of tight with. Problem with Daphnie is, Theena always gets the feeling Daphnie will sleep with a dude if she thinks he likes Theena on GP. There is always this underlining tinge of jealousy with Daphnie when it comes to her friends. Like when one of Daphnie's best friends Stephanie got married. All Daphnie did the entire wedding ceremony was complain that Stephanie had just cheated on her soon to be hubby and that they didn't belong together. Daphnie had just separated from her fiancé and was bitter about anyone else having a relationship. From the beginning Daphnie was the sleep around kind and how that engagement came about was a mess scheduled for a separation even sooner than the completion date. Daphnie had skipped school all in high school and had Theena come with her while she slept with guys at different guys houses. One time the one guy's mother was home when Daphnie and Theena went to his house. The mother just sat there watching her soaps while Theena sat on the couch across from her waiting on Daphnie. Daphnie had gotten pregnant five times by the time they finished high school. At each abortion she had called Theena to drive her home. After college Daphnie was still a Fertile Mertile and had four kids by three different men.

"Hi," Theena greets Daphnie. Theena stands up and walks over to where Daphnie is sitting with a few guys Daphnie works with and one not so attractive chick. Daphnie is insulted since Theena hasn't introduced her to Daniel. She asked to spend the night at his house one time when she was going to be in California but Theena's brand new acting ass came up with every excuse in the book before finally screaming a flat out, "HELL NO!"

Theena had had a mentally abusive relationship with a dude she very well had no business being with and Daphnie had been there for her when he had sent a crew of hoodrat girls to beat Theena down which is why Daphnie is not at all happy about this shit with Theena. It's like she's embarrassed of Daphnie now or something. And Theena wouldn't even have met her lil' NFL boyfriend had Daphnie not taught Theena how to do her weave and makeup!

Daphnie looks Theena up and down real harsh and critical when she thinks Theena is not looking but Theena catches it in peripheral. Theena looks different. A little darker brown, a lot slimmer. Talks different—more proper-like. She has a real hot, long weave and she's dressed a lot better than she had last year. Even that one time when Theena came to town she was dressed rather raggedy. Tonight, she looks like a football player's girlfriend. Finally.

Daphnie feels Theena should have introduced her to that brown skinned dude at their table who was solo. So what if she has a boyfriend? Who knows what Daphnie's dude does in his free time!

"Hey, Kwame," Theena introduces herself to one of the guys she remembers Daphnie saying she kind of liked. He holds her hand a longer than necessary and licks his lips. "If you wasn't already taken—um, um, umph!" He shakes his head with lament. Theena remembers the time he tried to talk to her. Even though Daphnie had a dude, she took off her sweater, put her extra big breasts all in Kwame's face and made sure he didn't say shit else to Theena the rest of the night. Good thing anyway. He was nice looking but he wasn't exactly Theena's type. Theena's a bit artsy. Although she usually has a classy way about herself, she's still one of those tree huggers and a bit eccentric. Kwame is clearly more hood. There was another time even before that when he had tried to holler at Theena and Daphnie sat in the middle of them on the couch at his house and made sure she broke that shit up.

Theena shakes the other dude's hand—Jerrit, the one who is cute but kind of funny looking—looks like a cute faced, little skinny-headed gecko. Daphnie's told Theena more than a few times that she can tell he has a big dick. His name was always coming up in conversations with Daphnie who had an elementary crush. It was Jerrit this, Jerrit that. The one time Jerrit had flirted with Theena Daphnie dogged him to Theena on the phone the next night talking about how he wasn't really all that and only chicks that didn't have shit were on his ass. Daphnie, who thinks she is smarter and classier than everyone else, has no clue Theena and mostly everyone else has peeped her 'ghetto girl in the hood looking down from her thrown' syndrome.

After saying a few hellos, Theena goes back to the table and motions for Kymberly to come with. They are all cracking up at the table talking about something and Kymberly is reluctant to go but goes anyway. Kymberly's dark hair sways against her butt and she has a really nice shape, real thick legs, hips, a bubble booty with a little waist and is Greek. Everyone in the small restaurant stop to gawk and salivate in slow motion as the girls go to the restroom.

When Daphnie enters the restroom Theena is doing the most--dancing and bopping up and down and talking in a heavy fake accent she's really good at imitating as she careens and primps in front of the full-length mirror. Kymberly laughs so hard she can't breath and is holding on to the sink for support. With these two still acting like this, no wonder they say thirty is the new twenty.

Theena gets a text from Daniel to hurry up and come back since the waiter is there to take their dinner orders. Daphnie thinks they are leaving because she walked in. "Good to see you Daph," Theena rushes as she gives Daphnie a hug. Kymberly is busy looking over Daphnie with disgust. Since when did open mid-drift gut hanging out become in style? Kym tosses Daphnie a look that lets Daphnie know she thinks she is authentically low class even though Theena has never even mentioned a thing about Daphnie to Kym.

"You know her?" Kym questions before they go back to the table with their guys. Kym orders a salmon salad, Theena fried calamari while the guys each order a double serving of wings, fries and milkshakes. In an hour they will leave, visit one of Zabar's buddies from the home city's team and fly out of the city within the next three hours on the jet.

Theena feels as though she's finally learned from all her past failed relationships and has decided to keep people—her family, church and Daphnie--out of her business. Things have been much better ever since. She spends many mornings on her sweetie's yacht these days and shops in London at Harrods, flies to New York just for boutique shopping, works part-time with Kym at her handcrafted lingerie closet and Theena takes three acting classes a week—sometimes with private study in New

York and Daniel always makes sure she has a driver for her entire trip.

She hates that Daphnie probably feels as though she's fake now that she's with Daniel but he is *her* man—and they've been talking about marriage a lot lately. Daniel told her upfront when she first moved in with him that she'd have to leave the past alone. "I didn't get where I am now by hanging around low life type of muthafuckas or people not headed in the same direction. ...Everything is a path, baby. If you're headed for success, then you got to surround yourself with success and stay on that kind of path—adapt to a higher plane in life. A lot of those '*homegirls*' will be the same ones running to the press on you with shit or they will diss *you* if they are in *your* shoes. You don't have any kids yet and you have a promising career—don't let dead weight ruin *your* shit," he'd reminded her.

And she knows having Daphnie around very well might mess certain things up for her. Like the time Daphnie came to this one job Theena had a while back. Daphnie told security that Theena used to steal at 5-7-9 when they were in high school. After that, Assets Protection followed Theena around her entire shift and made it clear she should quit by giving her daily "routine security checks" wherein they'd take her bags and search them in front of all the other employees, they'd check her locker before and after her shift and all the other employees quit speaking to her. She'd go into the lunchroom at work and everyone would clear out seconds later. It got to the point where Theena couldn't take it, found another job and quit that one. There have been at least five times Theena tried to talk to

Daphnie about stuff like that but Daphnie being Daphnie, she'd snap on her and make Theena feel like a bad person.

Although Theena is almost certain Daniel would not hook up with Daphnie, something tells her not to bring her into her new circle. Theena likes her new life. It's nice to actually be around other people who have similar interest outside of talking about sex and clothes.

Kym's dad is a well know actor and Kym practically lives in the theater just like Theena. And Kym isn't going to go around telling everyone Theena's got an eating disorder. Now that Theena is watching her weight and isn't as thick as she used to be Daphnie has been going around telling people Theena is anorexic.

Daphnie hates this new 'Theena' she's now deemed 'a fake ass bitch who's forgotten where she came from.' But Theena is actually the same--only finally in her own element. Even more than that, what it comes down to--what it's been coming down to for a long, long time is that Theena is sick and tired of the way Daphnie used to always make rude remarks about her body and her family and the way Daphnie harasses her about not talking extra ratchet anymore. It's like ongoing sibling rivalry—only they're not siblings!

Theena can recall a many and a plenty occasions being around Daphnie and getting the feeling Daphnie had been bashing her to all her friends and family just like she bashed her family and her other girls to Theena. On two separate occasions, Daphnie has told Theena she thought Theena was very lazy. Theena could have been like "slut, hooker, skank, crook—sleeping with married men yourself and you wonder why you have such bad luck and aren't getting anywhere outside an EBT card"—but Theena held back and didn't say anything. Theena has heard some of the guys Daphnie's slept with dog the mess out of poor Daphnie. The way things have been going for Daphnie after she left Fred, her last baby's father, is one of the main reasons Theena'd encouraged her to get back with him; he was much better that than some of these other things that end up treating Daphnie like mere side booty. And Theena especially does not miss how Daphnie used to dog her when she was on her natural hair phase or how one time Daphnie had borrowed her brand new jeans and wore them without panties when she was on her period.

Then there was the time Daphnie tried to be bisexual. She lived in the strip clubs with that whack ass ex boyfriend Devin who was a small-time weed dealer.

And what about how Theena's ex, Andrew, hated Daphnie? Matter of fact, *all* of Theena's friends hated Daphnie. They said she was way too skanky.

And it seemed like Daph was always trying to tell Theena how to handle *her* relationships until they completely dissolved. But those few times Daphnie had man? Oh, she was a better than a butler around the house!

And all those crack drug dealers Daphnie had dated and bragged about—ugh. Drug dealing was so 1980's!

Daphnie, on the other hand, thinks it's just a matter of time before some shit goes wrong with Theena's little 'relationship,' which, to her, seems more like totalitarianism just like when she was with that dude who was a nut-case. Seems like Theena searches for men to control her. Now it's Daniel. Some time real soon she's gonna be crawling back trying to act like shit is still cool. How Theena just gone let somebody tell her who her friends should and shouldn't be? Theena got real quiet when she said she'd meet Theena out of town to try to help her write that grant for her acting non-profit company she just started. Instead Theena went and got some of Daniel's people to work with her on it and didn't let Daphnie help. What happened to looking out for your own? Daphnie feels like Theena knows Daphnie could very well use the money right about now.

Back in the day when Theena's broke ass didn't have shit but a part-time commission only telemarketing job, was laying around all day dreaming about an acting career, with a bunch of eviction notices on her door, she was the one that'd looked out for Theena and helped her pay some of her bills. She even let that bitch use her EBT food stamp card on more than a few occasions!

That one time she was in that acting school and dated that dumb, retarded boy that went around talking about Theena like a dog and fucked her chances of getting auditions, who was the one that had come to the school to shut them bitches hating on Theena down? Yep, the bitch she wants to turn her back on now!

And when Theena was skipping out on church and having flings with dudes from college, who was the one that still had her back and hung out with her when everyone else was saying she was "a cheap hoe"? *She* was the one that had taken up for Theena because she knew Theena's then fiancé was a liar and cheating from day one and

Theena had only been "wildin' out" for a minute because she was hurt by her fiancé.

And what about that lil' stripper stunt! Hell, Daphnie had never cheated on her guys like Theena had! But now this goody-goody, who had saved her virginity for marriage until college (she gave up that dream), who was immature and too afraid to suck her own boyfriend's dick back in the day was on the 'I'ma turn my back on the ones who done always had my back' shit. What about when everybody was saying Theena was weird? What about when Theena was looking skanky wit them damn dreads last year? Who still hung out with her forgetful ass and had her back?

Fuck *that*! Unless Theena calls her up and apologizes real soon, it is a wrap for *that* quote unquote friendship. Theena is supposed to be like a sister to her; Theena is supposed to be her children's godmother!

Fuck that bitch!

The Reapers

People usually wonder, when their lives don't turn out the way they planned or when they realize just how messed up their lives actually are, they usually wonder how they got from point A to point Z. Such is the case with David Richardson who used to dabble in the street pharmaceutical hustle and did his share of dirt back in the day but has since cleaned up his act.

It's still too late, though. The feds have finally gotten him. And he has exhausted his death row appeals. Next week, David Richardson, age 33 will be sent to the electrocution chair.

"Dat bitch still sleepin'?" Murl Lee asks pointing at the gorgeous golden skinned girl, surrounded in well past shoulder length braids a few covering her face like a daughter of Medusa, huddled in the thin, worn blanket.

"Man, fuck dat bitch. She think she can sleep away her time. She up in dis muthafucka just like all da rest of us. She ain't bedder dan no body," Murl Lee, a five-nine, two hundred and fifty-pound, red boned, wide nose, butchy looking chick in this time for raping another woman and eight charges of credit and identity fraud says. This is her third visit to prison.

"Y'all are being too hard on her, she's only twenty-one," a shorthaired, dark skinned forty something lady named Veronica remarks.

"I 'on't give a fuck! I know one thang: I'm 'bouta go in dat bitch bag and cop some of dat food her peeps sent yestaday," Murl Lee retorts.

Zanobia rolls over on the fingernail thin bunk mattress pretending not to hear. Nothing matters anyway. She's got at least eleven more years to do in here. If that goddamn Murl Lee takes all her shit, maybe she won't have to try to fight her off again tonight. Or maybe she'll starve to death and not have to do her fuckin' time. Unless her family or the church and her best friend send commissary, she does not eat. The cafeteria only serves murky slop with bread on the side. She is hoping to one day die soon-- hopefully two days from now or even today.

At five feet one, Zanobia now only weights eighty-nine pounds. Eventually her cellmates all leave and she covers her face with the stiff synthetic blanket trying to shut off all the fart and Ammonium smells in the cell and in the hallway from seeping back into her dreams and she goes back to sleep.

A little later, Veronica comes in. "Nobie? Nobie? Sweetie, you need to get up. We're going outside in a few minutes... Come outside and get some fresh air... I know you hear me... Nobie?" Zanobia turns her head to face the wall. "When you wake up, you're still gonna be here, honey. You just a baby. You gone have to make peace with whatever got you in here. You gone have to find you some sort of happiness... Come on."

Zonobia opens her eyes and looks down at the lady. Veronica's smile reminds her of her aunt Susan's smile—a small gap, stiff but sincere nonetheless. She forces herself to stand. She is woozy.

"That come from not eating, chile. Come on."

"V? V!" a chick with a freshly incised tattoo of what is probably her child's name inscribed on her forearm calls to Veronica. Instead of going out side, Veronica goes into the TV room with the rest of the inmates on Zanobia's floor. The television is so old the lady sitting only a ruler's length away from it is using a hanger to change the channels.

"Look at dis nigga right here! Dis shit don't make no sense! If *I* was out there, I'd get my ass right back up in here dealin' wit a shitty ass muhfuka like *his* ass!" a woman named Melissa shouts and everyone shouts back in agreement. Zanobia goes in and sits down next to Veronica. This will be the first time in three months she's watched television. She's been in a women's facility in Plymouth, Michigan for five months and is already looking for a way to escape. She was supposed to be at Ferris State University right now. She would have taken the PCAT test and next fall she would have entered the college of pharmacy.

All that money her parents spent in high school on SAT/ACT tutorials and out of pocket to cover the ten thousand dollars her scholarship didn't cover at Ferris...all that and now this.

Zanobia stops rehashing the thoughts that run thru her mind twenty-four seven and catches a glimpse of the show that has everyone ranting and raving in the TV room—if you could call it a TV room. *Real Divorce Court*. Zanobia stands up ready to finally go outside but instead turns around to face the voice that has now stopped her heart.

It is David. David. The one who told her to hold his gun "right quick." The one who took off when the police arrived on the scene. The one left her out there with the fingerprints to be found guilty.

DAVID. Her first and only, the one she'd skipped eighth hour World History for every Friday. Mrs. Bryant, her high school band instructor, had warned her every time he'd come to pick her up from practice. But she hadn't listened. Her grandmother said she was hard headed…

The one she hadn't been allowed to go to prom with and ended up missing prom completely since he wasn't going for her taking another dude to prom. The one who'd almost made her get kicked off campus when he drove all the way up to her school and clowned on her because she had tried to end the relationship.

Him.

"Nobie, I 'on't never ask you fa nothin' why cain't you just come down here wit me right quick," he'd said. *Don't date that low budget thug. You weren't raised to hook up with rift-raft, Nobie. You came from a good family for heaven's sakes!* Four years with that mess—what everybody and their mama called a low life. Everyone had warned her but she hadn't listened.

Not even a year later and he is on *Real Divorce Court*! Come to find out, he's been married for two years to this slightly older looking, attractive woman. Kelly Richardson.

"Your honor, this man wouldn't even take me to the hospital when I was *in labor*!" the Kelly lady huffs.

"I had told her the day before that if she didn't get a better paying job, I wasn't about to do nothing foe her, Yo' Honor! The bills was due and she wasn't doing nothing but digging all in my pockets."

The judge rolls her eyes then stops and demands David look at his wife, she demands that he look at the pain covering her face.

"Your Honor, this man yelled at me in the middle of the restaurant so bad because I didn't have enough to pay the bill—and I was nine months pregnant at the time, mind you—that two guys from the next table over asked me if they could help. And he was too much of a punk *to say anything to them*." She pauses and chokes down tears. "And like a dummy, I still went home with him. And you know what, Your Honor? He had the nerve to punch me in the stomach after we left the restaurant!"

David laughs. "It sound like I was just straight up jabbin' her and whatnot—that ain't how it all went down. I smacked her—I ain't punch her in the stomach—everybody was tellin' me the kid wasn't mine--I wasn't gone be taking care of another dude's seed. And I felt like she shoulda checked them dudes fa—"

Never mind the paternity test, which proves 99 point whatever percent Kelly Richardson's son is David Richardson's as well. Whatever else happens on that television, whatever else anyone says or does, does not matter. Zanobia starts screaming and screaming and screaming and bites Murl Lee's fist when she comes over to punch Zanobia for not shutting the fuck up so everybody could finish watching the show. She will not stop screaming in a scornful rage, biting and kicking everyone coming towards her until almost an hour later when they take her into the ward and medicate her.

David has never written to Zanobia, sent commissary…he has not accepted any of her calls. Until today, she was certain he'd been caught and in prison and didn't know how to contact her. Or either dead. Those were the only excuses. That was how she'd managed to forgive him and partially herself for the situation. She hadn't known he'd gone and blown a girl's brains out and had *her* sitting in the front seat of the car while he'd done it.

In court he had the whole story set—his boys, his aunt—even his grandmother vouched for his story—his lie that he hadn't been out with Zanobia on that fateful day. They even conjured up a big cover up—that she was jealous of the girl and thought David was cheating on her with the girl. And that Zanobia had gotten him confused with his now incarcerated identical twin, Donathan who was out at the time. Don had a record long enough. There wasn't any proof nor detectable reason for David to have killed LaNae Jenkins. They'd found Zanobia guilty fair and square. One of the girl's neighbors testified that she'd seen Zanobia walk around the side of the girl's house. But that was only because David had called her—on his burned-out phone. He'd told her to "come in for a second to meet his cousin but the minute she reached the stairs David had rushed Zanobia off the porch and into the car."

When Dr. McDonald, who has resigned from her position as Area F superintendent and is now on heavy prescribed anti-depressants and ECT's, hears that her daughter is in the psychiatric ward, her husband, Dr. McDonald, has to shut down his veterinary office and rush his wife to the hospital after coming home and finding his wife sitting in front of the vanity mirror in her bathroom holding a butcher's knife limply against her chest with vacant eyes.

In the separate unit Zanobia's entire body from her lips to her toes tremble and quiver and she continues in her refusal to eat. Instead she thinks about it and thinks about it…and thinks about it—the day David drove to that girl's house. She goes over and over it until the male nurse comes in to inject the syringe into her left hip on schedule.

When the married male nurse thinks Zanobia is completely knocked out, he unzips Zanobia's strapped white suit that has replaced her orange prison's uniform and uncuffs the handcuffs locking her to her bed. The male nurse does everything he's ever wanted to do to a woman until he checks his watch and realizes they will soon be paging and looking for him.

Too bad this chick is crazy and up in here—she sexy as hell, he thinks already planning to come back tomorrow for more. Usually only female nurses can do one-on-one's but the entire week they have been short staffed. Quite frankly, nobody's rushing to work in Plymouth when they can get paid just as much in a regular hospital where they don't have to worry about all the shit that goes on in prisons. Just like the inmates are locked in, the workers are locked inside too.

A week later and Zanobia is still a screamer and unwilling to speak to anyone and unwilling to eat completely now. She does not even read the letter her father has sent.

Instead, Zanobia fakes sleep once again when the male nurse arrives—one who will soon be bloodstained deep within the molecules of his spirit. She rolls over as he finishes. The male nurse is so afraid of being caught he rushes out without completely zipping her back up and cuffing her to the side of the bed properly. Even though he doesn't want to get busted, he thinks it would be a shame to waste a piece like this.

The next morning when the male nurse does his rounds prior to signing off third shift, he stops by to see Zanobia. She acts normal and calm this time.

After two weeks of calm behavior, Zanobia is reintegrated back to her cell with Murl Lee and Veronica where the male nurse cannot get to her. The first day back in her cell during lunch in the lunchroom, Zanobia starts a fight with Murl Lee and her posse by telling Murl Lee not to touch the food her family sends her. Murl Lee, who is used to doing as she pleases and still sour Zanobia bit her on the knuckles, cannot believe Zanobia has stood up to her a second time.

"What? What? You wanna be Tough Tone up in here, na?" a heavy handed Murl Lee asks thrashing

Zanobia's head into the metal lunch table four times. The six chicks in Murl Lee's posse jump in and start kicking and punching every inch of Zanobia they can reach splitting her lip and breaking her nose. Zanobia does not fight back.

Once she is completely laid out on the floor Murl Lee commands four of the girls to stomp Zanobia until they get tired. Soon she can no longer feel the kicks in the chest.

By the time the guards arrive on the scene, Zanobia's scull and two ribs are cracked and she is no longer breathing.

It was either starve to death or find a quicker way out. This was the only way Zanobia figured she could end her bad situation.

Norletta McDonald, even high on her meds and uppers, has been pondering quite a few things since Zanobia's trial. Like how her ex-husband, Samson McDonald, caught her with his brother Samuel. She had told Samson she wasn't feeling well and was leaving church early. He'd decided to order from the Rattlesnake and bring dinner home instead of taking Pastor and First Lady out as they'd planned since Norletta quote unquote wasn't feeling well. When Samson arrived home early it was a while before Norletta and Samuel realized Samson was standing in the doorway with emerald-burgundy eyes. Norletta, partially shamed from being caught but not really, smirked, got up and told Samson he needed to leave—"if he hadn't been a one minute brotha none of this shit would have happened," she taunted as he raced down the stairs in silence—the screeching tires being the only break in Samson's silence.

Samson, who had recently passed away without knowing of Norletta's recent suffering, had long since moved somewhere in the UK. She'd heard from someone at church that he had moved and taught as an economics Professor at a university there. He never remarried or had children, Norletta had heard from someone, who, coincidentally Samson had worked with, who had never known Samson had been married. Such a small world these days. And Norletta had never apologized or even talked to him since the day he caught her with Samuel. Samson had never stepped foot in their house again after the day she told him to leave.

Samson had paid all her educational loans off and they never fought like she and Samuel sometimes did. Once Samuel and her had fought so bad, her eye stayed purple for almost two weeks.

Anytime Norletta thinks about Zanobia, she thinks about all of this.

Zanobia was Samuel McDonald's little princess--his one and only. He will never forgive himself for allowing any of this to happen to her. He tried, he really did, to be the best father. Shenise, his first wife who divorced him after finding out about him and Norletta, had a stillbirth shortly after she'd found out--a son they were going to name Malcolm Samson McDonald.

Good thing he'd managed to talk Norletta out of the abortion she had scheduled when she found out she was pregnant with Nobie. But she had gone and gotten her tubes tied right after Nobie and hadn't told him until after he had wasted all that money on tests and the trip to California to see all those infertility specialists. He got so angry he hauled off and downright beat the crap out of her. One thing about Shenise, she had wanted a house full of babies and would have made a good homemaker. All Norletta cared about was her next promotion.

Then there were the check scams that, as of lately, kept running thru his mind. The upwards of three-hundred and sixty thousand dollars. And he had never been caught—Norletta had done a good job of keeping her mouth shut about it. But ever since Zanobia was brutally beaten to death, he had an insurmountable urge to right all those wrongs.

David Richardson at this time, it seemed, was living his life. David moved to Texas and was already living with another chick before his divorced was finalized and only appeared to be like any other regular jerk--nothing extra atrocious; just a flat-out, no good, jerk, that's all. But he finally changed. By this time David had learned from the mistakes he had made in the past.

The new one he fell in love with, however, was quite the joke.

He found out that his son by her was not his five years later (because he trusted her and never pressed for a paternity test--unlike he had with Kelly). David had two other kids by his lady love that he took care of like a real stand up guy, a daughter who was shot right in front of him while riding her tricycle down the block, the other, three year old Lacey, who suffered a stroke and was diagnosed with Leukemia.

Although he was a faithful deadbeat dad when it came to his two sons by Kelly, David had a decent office job, he made around thirty-thousand. Everyone at work loved him and David was only a semester away from graduating as a computer's study major with honors when the cops arrived in the hallway of his classroom. The local new stations and their camera crew were outside ready to expose the story.

Years later the investigation team, with all their new technology, attained a tip from the Crime Hotline and traced his phone from way back in the day which proved that he was in fact at LaNae's house on the day of her murder.

Ulonda, the girl he was already living with before he and Kelly had divorced, Ulonda, whose car note and rent he had been paying from day one, Ulonda who had given him a permanent atrocious case of herpes will never come to visit, never write and block collect calls from her phone.

Ulonda, "who ain't got no time fa no nigga who gone be gitin' his ass blew out every night," plans on moving to Denver with her first son's father next week.

No one from David Richardson's family will make it to his execution.

The Other Woman—1 PSO's Life

Brenda is depressed. Like, depressed, *depressed*. Once she hit four hundred and ten pounds in April she stopped caring. Her last boyfriend, Bob, an excruciatingly skinny, red neck truck driver with a bad case of Psoriasis who has a passion for "big cunts," ran off with Dawn—the chain smoking brunette chick downstairs that wore pink foundation, green sparkley eye shadow and had four kids all with different men. (One of the dudes still came by and "got nasty" from time to time with Dawn and Bob knew but never said anything about it). Bob and Dawn had moved across the yard-way of Brenda's apartment complex and went to every apartment community event with no shame. Bob was now doing local truck gigs. The whole year he had been with Brenda he had been doing 'cross country drives that usually left him only three days in Michigan with Brenda a month. After the first two months of their relationship, he had only called an hour a week and whenever he came into town, he'd spent the entire time at The Higgins Hole In The Wall buying drinks for all the hot young lookers and his new male buddies for the night.

Bob had been the only boyfriend Brenda ever had since high school. In the glorious high school days, she had been on the volleyball and cheer team and a prom queen nominee. But things had changed for many reasons that summer of '98. Things were never the same after those girls put that stuff in her drink at prom.

There was no proof. Brenda still thought there should have been a way to sue or to do something. But she had just kept it all to herself. No need to make a big deal. She had always been nice. Things like that didn't happen to nice girls that everyone liked who'd gotten straight A's. Things like that weren't supposed to go down in Warren, Michigan in the late 90's. Now in her late thirties, what was once a luscious head of bleached blonde mall hair was now a thinning butt length crop topped with barely-there bangs. And the hairs on her jaw-line and chin were doing a good job of getting fuller and darker. She thought about laser but what was the use? Too bad she couldn't switch the hairs on her chin with the ones on her head—that's what the kids in 16B had teased last week when she came back from grocery shopping.

Brenda only goes out once a week. She usually gets everything done on Wednesdays. Groceries, the dollar store, sometimes the post office. Now that they deliver groceries she may just start staying in. These days with, internet and wifi and all, she really doesn't have a desire to go anywhere. Especially with the way all the neighbors in her building watch and pick at her and laugh and laugh. Why are people so mean? The Black chick with the purple and black weave that sits like a hat on her head is an Ashley Stewart's shopper no doubt and her son is rather plump for a ten year old. But even she whispers with her next door neighbor Pat when they catch her coming up the two flights of stairs out of breath. Brenda does her best to take her garbage out at night. And even then, there is usually someone up watching and saying rude things out of the dark windows.

This is one of the three reasons she likes her job. As a phone sex operator she gets good payback. First of all, the neighbors below her and next door can hear. The apartment walls are pretty thin. It really pisses them off to hear her making all those "OOOh, yes! Harder, harder!" cooing remarks. They can't figure out exactly what it is she is doing. They've even called the police on her twice and when they came, there was no one inside except Brenda.

She's been doing this PSO gig for seventeen years now and is pretty darned good at it. She only does regular customers at this point, averages thirty-five dollars per hour and is especially good at domination. It feels good to telling men that sound like Bob to suck her toes harder and to tie up their dicks with shoe strings. She tells them she can tell if they are faking or not—they especially love that. Sometimes they send her extra money to her P.O. Box. Pictures. Four guys email and instant message her regularly and most men say they fall in love with her the minute they hear her voice. She sounds exactly like Marilyn Monroe a quirky sounding guy from Rhode Island always says. He does something in the IT field that enables him to send Brenda five hundred dollars each month. One time his wife picked up the phone. Brenda played it smooth and abruptly quit gargling Pepsi in her mouth like she was swallowing his cum and quit spanking her ass for him. The wife was severely angry. "You don't even look at me anymore! You don't even spend money on your kids' school clothes! You weasel! Frank you weasel, you!" It was the way her voice shrieked, the shrillness of her words. Brenda laughed a little. She sounded like she'd gone to some high fla-lutin' college. Like a Priss Pot who was too frigid to do anything outside of missionary. His wife probably looked like one of those girls who had doctored up her drink.

The thrill for Brenda was when Frank, who she'd only ever known as her "Little Pussy Boy," refused to end his call with her. Brenda could hear his wife in the background crying and screaming like a defeated skinny angel. She just sounded skinny to Brenda. Skinny bitches always have the scratchiest voices.

Then there is Dave who has called her every day faithfully for the last ten years. He had begged her to meet up with him before he married his ex wife. Brenda knew, from all the stories he'd told her—especially the story about when he had taken Cheryl to Aspen and she stayed inside the cabin the entire vacation because Dave hadn't let her bring her dog Charmy along--Brenda knew it wasn't going to work. For as long as Brenda had been talking to Dave he said he wanted kids but Cheryl had told him *Charmy*—who had his own bedroom and bathroom along with television and daybed—was child enough! Brenda always wonders why such nice men like Dave always pick such terrible Prima Donna hoochies. Currently Dave is dating a new girl—same name—Cheryl only spelled differently—Cherrald. A mix between her parents' names Cherrie and Ronald. This one is just like the first Cheryl. All fluff and looks—the typical Diva Bitch. He says she comes from money and is a sweetheart but she won't give him oral to save his life. Sometimes Dave asks Brenda to simulate blow jobs for him but he usually starts talking instead. Brenda knows all about the guys at work Dave hangs out at the bar with when he tells Cherrald he's doing overtime. She knows which manager Dave is planning on firing next week. She knows how much money Cherrald spends on undies each month. She knows that Cherrald is double jointed and can put her foot on top of her head. She knows all about Cherrald's two best friends—Sindy and Ling. And Dave is very generous. He usually always sends Brenda monetary and other treats each month. Once, after his divorce with the first Cheryl, he sent Brenda the ring Cheryl'd left behind then harassed him for in court. A blazingly clear solitaire set in platinum. And there was the diamond necklace for Christmas last year. There was only one time Dave didn't send her something. In February. And that was only because the new Cherrald had depleted his account, Dave said.

Brenda knows Dave is the kind that won't even look cashiers at Meijer's who look like her in the eye—that Dave is the kind that wipes his hands after handing his money over to cashiers that look like her.

Then there is Vinnie who is gay and unhappy about it. He just cannot come to terms with the fact that he wishes his penis were smaller and two lipped with a clit stuck in between. He also wishes he could convince his best friend Marsago to kiss him and "play around" with him. But Vinnie tried tapping Marsago's butt once and Marsago punched him and told him he "didn't get down like that, man!" "It wasn't on purpose!" Vinnie protested. "Still, man! I don't play dat shit!" Marsago insisted.

With Vinnie Brenda pretends to be Marsago or any other boy Vinnie is crushing hard on. That usually last an hour. Then after that, they usually talk another thirty minutes about favorite TV shows before Vinnie sends her fake kisses good-bye.

These are the best fourty-five hours of her week. The rest of the time Brenda watches television, sleeps longer than sixteen hours the days she doesn't work and drinks the gallon of 151 straight from the bottle because she can handle it, right before she cries herself to sleep. There are yellow hostess cupcakes in bed with her. Two loaves of pita bread are in the bed with her. Three packages of pastrami. A couple of empty Pepsi two liter bottles. Oreos bought in bulk from Costco's. A bulk jar of Jiffy peanut butter. Cooked Kielbasa. The Jerky Turkey cradles her neck. She hasn't brushed her teeth for most of the month or taken a bath or a shower in three days. Lately watching *The View* and *Jerry Springer* and the mesh of reality shows doesn't do it anymore—doesn't make the time not talking to her favorite guys go by any faster. More and more she is starting to eat and drink liquor in bed.

It's okay, she tells herself. *It's okay*. And she thinks about how Bob had tried to auction her off on that one escort website. No one bid. She wonders if someone would have bid if he would still be calling her on Mondays or coming over once or twice a month…

Dachelle, Dachelle...Dachelle From Hell

"FUCK YOU, SHORT ASS, DUMB ASS, MUTHAFUCKA!" Dachell screams at her husband Dana when he enters the house at four in the morning. Before he cheated, she didn't mind what time he came in. Now, since that hood ass rat showed up at her door and told her what Dana had been up to, things have changed. "MATTER FACT, I'M BETTER THAN YOU, YOU BASTARD!" With that she spits on Dana. "I GOT ALL THESE MEN TALKIN' ABOUT HOW GOOD OF A WOMAN I AM AND I'M UP HERE DEALIN' WIT YO' BULLSHIT!"

Dana is wiping the spit off his forehead when a butcher knife dashes past the temple of his forehead and hits the wall. He missed being sliced across the ear with it by a centimeter. Dana doesn't fight back as Dachelle continues to call him every name imaginable and gets in his face. He just stands there thinking about how he should have stayed out even later.

In the midst of it all, their three-year old daughter little Dana wakes up crying.

"SEE WHAT YOU DID—YA BITCH! YOU WOKE DANA UP! I HATE YOU! I HATE YO' TRIFLIN' ASS!" Dachelle screams just as enraged as she was twenty minutes ago.

"He's a BITCH!" Dachelle tells her longtime girlfriend Mya the next day on the phone after Dana has left for work. "From now on when he comes in late that's what he's gonna have to deal with. I don't even know why I put up wit that short, lil dick muthafucka's shit anyway."

"You can't do that, Dachelle. Why don't you two go for counseling? You two can probably work things out. Dana doesn't seem like that bad of a guy, girl. Lemme tell you, *my* ex husband? Oh, he woulda nutted up on your ass and tried to break your neck. You done broke the poor man's finger and everything else. Why don't you try to move past this? Lots of couples are able to maintain a good marriage after one incident of infidelity. It's not like he's still cheating."

"Shit, he could be. Seems like he woulda had his ass in early after a bitch comes and tells on 'im. I could be with a man with more money, that's fine and tall instead of dealing with this Dana shit. Yesterday he pissed me off so bad, I locked him out. He sat in his car for two hours—looked like he went to sleep. Then I heard a loud noise and got up outta bed. He had kicked a dent in the front door. So I finally opened the door and let him in. But, I mean, we got to arguing so bad, he locked himself in the bedroom and I busted the door down. Aw! It was WWF on that bitch!"

Mya thinks Dachelle is pretty, has a lot going for her and all but she really hopes Dachelle can get past this. It's all they ever talk about. One day Dachelle and Dana are arguing, the next day they've had sex and everything seems to be fine. It's up one day then it's down the next day. Just when you think they are going to get a divorce, they start getting along. The minute you think the frenzy has calmed down once and for all, they're fighting all over again. Well, Dachelle is fighting while Dana just sits back and takes it.

The next thing about it is, Dachelle has cheated on Dana in order to pay him back but she still doesn't think they are even.

"He thinks I'm just supposed to get over it. So look, he can take my shit, nah! You cheat, you get beat," Dachelle laughs.

"Well...go to counseling and see what happens. But you should try to stop beating him up, Dachelle. If a man was doing all the stuff you do to him to a woman, it would be considered domestic violence."

"Well he's a thug-hoodlum. And his family are nothing but a bunch of drug addicts. I don't know. Maybe the way he was raised makes Dana act like this. His mama wasn't a good mother... My family wasn't like that. None of us are on drugs."

Mya hopes Dachelle will go talk to a professional because things with Dachelle are getting out of hand. The thing about the whole situation that's really starting to bother Mya is that Dachelle doesn't ever seem to think she's done anything to Dana or anyone. She talks about his family something terrible but when they're around she's nothing but nice to them. As much junk as she talks about Dana's mom, she let her live with them before she died of cancer and allowed his drug addicted brother and sister live with them in the past, too. She's talked about her own family, as well. There's her drug-addicted aunt who never moved out of her grandmother's house and used to use to poop in the basement sink. There's the severely alcoholic uncle. Her cousins that had sex in her parent's garage—all of whom Dachelle finds beneath her. But she still invites them to get-togethers at her house and acts friendly towards them at family outings. To see her with her family, they would never guess she's said such things about them.

And she talks about her friends. Called Jazmeen's baby ugly. Said the guy she cheated on Dana with, Alton, was fat, gross and ugly—looked like Barney. She's harshly critical of everyone except herself. Mya has even heard Dachelle talk about her once when she thought Mya had hung up the phone. None of Dachelle's friends can stand each other because of the things she says about them behind their backs.

"I might go to counseling with him but what I probably need is another man. He had all this at home and went to that rat. I keep looking at her Facebook picture and can't believe how ugly she is. I'm better than her," Dachelle says.

"Well…you should have taken out some of your anger on that girl for coming to your house with that mess. You keep taking everything out on Dana but that girl deserved to get knocked out for coming to your door like that." Mya still can't understand how Dachelle can scream at Dana and beat him up but let that girl slide. "If she would have come to *my door* I would have invited her in and commenced to whipping her behind—and I don't even like to fight!"

"I was shocked and sort of relieved. I wasn't thinking about fighting her. I was kinda glad she told me they had been sleeping together because it let me know I wasn't crazy. I had been feeling like he was cheating all that time and he kept denying it."

"Yeah…but you said she came to your house again after that. You've got to stop that chick from thinking she can just pop up at your crib…"

"I'm not really worried about her. I'm married to him! He's the one that fucked up! Yesterday I went to his job and knocked two paint cans over on his desk when he ain't bring his ass home. All his papers fell on the floor—aw, I tell you. Paint was everywhere. I started to go and key some of the cars he was working on too but I didn't. I fucked him up! He got all mad! Man was he pissed. But he ain't do shit! Nigga know not to do shit! If he knew how to act, I wouldn't have to attack his dumb ass… Sometimes I think he thinks I'm lazy or something because I haven't gone in to work for the last month. I saw him the other day looking at me when I was watching TV. Shit, they let me work from home. And he doesn't have to worry about where I'm at. I usually have my ass at home. But not *this* muthafucka! Staying out til three in the morning and shit. Next time he come in that late I'ma tackle his ass!" Dachelle laughs.

"**Me and Dana went** to counseling today. He was cool--a Black guy. He was saying how these thots are getting more and more trifling nowadays. He told Dana he's lucky to have a good woman like me… After two more weeks of couples therapy Dana is going to go to sessions on his own to deal with his issues. I think he changed after his mother died.

That's when he stopped paying the bills and started hanging out in the streets all the time."

Actually Mya can remember when Dana wasn't working and Dachelle was paying all the bills back in the day but says nothing about that. Dana probably was going thru grief from his mother's death that he probably hadn't dealt with but there is more than just that going on.

"Did you address the fighting?" Mya asks being careful how she phrases it. It's more like Dana getting his ass beaten really.

"Naw, we didn't even bring that up to the counselor."

After session two, Dana quits going to counseling. Dachelle has lost her job and she and Mya are no longer friends.

One day Dachelle ran into one of Mya's ex boyfriends and had given him Mya's new phone number much to Mya's consternation. "Oh, whatever. Get over it. I did it now, so what!" Dachelle yelled at Mya when Mya told her she hadn't appreciated her giving her number to that clown.

A week later Mya thought Dachelle would at least apologize about it since the whole situation, Dachelle giving out her number and yelling at her, had made her uncomfortable. "I don't understand how you can yell at me, but you couldn't say shit when your husband's jumpoff came knocking on your door," Mya says, sincerely hurt.

"Well you're more stupid than his jumpoff and you can lose my number, you stupid bitch! You're just jealous of me! I hope you have a bad life and lots of voodoo to your ass! All you do is talk about the past and your ex husband and you need to get a real job instead of talking 'bout you in school! Get off yo' lazy ass! I knew I shoulda listened to Dana. He never liked yo' stupid ass! I see why yo' ex husband cheated on you!" Dachelle yells.

"Well you have a good life and live well," Mya replies. That tidbit of information just confirmed that Dachelle thought she was better than her; to think someone is jealous of you, you'd have to think they were beneath you. Mya wonders how she could ever be jealous of all the drama Dachelle had going on.

"I'm gone have a good life. Can't say the same for you! I won't miss ya, either! You talk too damn much, tell all yo' business and don't appreciate shit!" Dachelle insist on having the last word.

Unlike Dana, Mya walks away. There is a difference between friends and spouses.

Like Garden Eyes

Blood

"**Take it off!** *Ta-ta-ta-take* it off, Black Adonis!" Maxine chants sing song at the ebony skinned, massive muscles Adonis in a navy, extra fitted policeman's uniform now undulating and gyrating in front of her. "Thank you, Tavia!" She takes her eyes off the stripper for a few seconds, turns to her best friend and holds her drink up in a toast.

"Yeah, and you ain't want no stipper! Girl, *please*!" Octavia responds.

"The only dick you ever got and *gone git* nah is Tally so we wanted to give you a lil' sumthen, sumthen *ta savor and enjoy*!" TaChandra chimes in.

Kandy, Nicolette and Ema all grope the fake policeman.

"Get away! He's mine!" Maxine shouts smiling as he leisurely removes his shirt. Kandy takes the shirt and rubs it all over her chest.

"We got the whole night ta *par-tay*!" Ema shouts over the music walking away from the hotel bed to the mini bar to pour another cosmopolitan from the silver shaker. "Now, I'm not one ta drink, but Kandy, you sho know how to make a *drank*!" she adds.

The next morning everything is hazy and Maxine has a harrowing sensation traveling from her head to her toes. She can't find her other shoe, every fifteen minutes she feels like she's got to throw up again, she's three hours late to her hair appointment and her wedding is in four hours.

"Liza is pissed off. She said she had to cancel three of her other regulars but she's still willing to do your hair *so hurry up, Max*! She's going to be at the apartment in an hour," Octavia says coming from the next door, adjoining suite.

"This is all y'alls fault! Y'all *know* I don't drink!" Maxine sputters.

"Well, you had a good time, didn't you—Ms. I Don't Go Nowhere!" Octavia replies.

"Yeah, yeah… Whatever. I wish we could do this tomorrow," Maxine says.

"Well, today's the day! Today is the day we don't have to be roommates anymore—I love you, girl but it's been seven years of me having to listen to your drama with Tally everyday! Do you know what that's like? From now on I'll be living by myself—Tally Talk-Free Days—thank ya' Jesus!" Octavia says teasingly. Actually, they had all thought it would be her and Mason getting married before Tally and Max. But Octavia is not green-eyed or envious of her friend. Tally and Max had had so many issues. But Tally had man-ed up and was finally ready to say "I Do."

Mason, once Mr. Perfect, had left Octavia for some white stripper he'd met in Vegas. He was supposed to be on a three day trip with the fellas. Two days into his trip Mason, had called Octavia, told her he had met someone and had gotten married and then politely told her he was taking *all* the money in his and Octavia's joint savings account. What a way to end a five year relationship!

At least one of us is getting married. I'm gonna miss my girl but she deserves to be happy. Max is a good girl. Octavia thinks as she hands over the room keys to the front desk attendant and checks out of the hotel. *This is going to be a long day*, Octavia sighs. Standing in the hotel lobby she can see Maxine in the parking lot opening the car door and throwing up.

Maxine's eyes are red and, as she stands at the altar, she's wishing she was wearing a pair of sunglasses. The ceremony looks as nice as planned and Tally is handsome but…well. He had been her one and only. Marriage. At twenty-six, after eight years of on-again off-again dating, Tally had moved out of town and then back in town, after all the constant productions between her and his bi-polar mother when she didn't take her medicine, they were finally getting married. Not to mention that one crazy chick Valerie. The one who claimed Tally was the father of her child. Had him and Maxine watching that boy on the weekends for almost two years before Tally found out Jamar was not his. After all that—now this; Maxine Irone becomes Maxine Lancaster. *Well, we made it, I guess… Lord, please let me be a good wife to Tally.* Right after her short prayer the preacher prompts Maxine to say her vows.

"How is he doc? What's my son's status?" Tally asks frantically. He and Maxine have been sitting in the

Children's Hospital waiting room for hours with barely any consolation from the intensive care unit.

"Tell us something! *Something!* You probably aren't a parent—if you were you'd be doing everything you could and you would tell us something! We need to know *something*!" Maxine pleads.

The doctor holds his hand in protest. In cases like these nothing he can say will ease the minds of the parents. "He's going to need a blood transfusion, Mrs. Lancaster. The injury that has incurred due to the blow has caused internal bleeding," the doctor informs them. "Do either of you happen to know your blood types? That could speed up things…" he adds.

"A blood transfusion? Lord, Lord, Lord. I shouldn't have let him play. How can a kid get injured this bad from a simple game of baseball? It's all my fault! I should—"

"—Maxine, stop it! We don't have time for all of that right now. Let's take care of this." Tally says to his wife before turning his attention back to the doctor. "I don't know my blood type but—"

"--I don't know mine either! But you've got to do something fast, doctor!" Maxine interjects.

It takes three nurses to finally calm Maxine down enough to test her blood. The entire time Maxine is thinking and thinking. Thinking about how she and Tally met. Thinking about how he'd proposed. Then thinking about how much fun they had their wedding night. Their honeymoon flight to Jamaica had been delayed so they stayed in a cheap hotel near the airport. That night for the first time Tally had cum in her without a condom. That's when she knew she was his and he was hers. Prior to that he had always used condoms. That was one of the reasons she'd thought he had been a total dummy when it came to that Valerie situation. He'd sworn he had used a condom with Valerie and was shocked but presumed his role as a father when Valerie had told him.

Tally is a take-care-of-business kind of guy. That was one of the things Maxine loved about him. He hadn't gotten mad when she found out she was pregnant a month and a half after the wedding. Maxine had been pissed about it—back then she hadn't wanted kids. But the look in Tally's eyes when he found out, that had sort of softened her heart towards the thought of a baby. Tally had been so good to her the entire pregnancy taking the petty arguments she constantly started, rubbing her achy swollen feet, making her feel better about her ever stretching stomach and marks. The only thing he'd really argued back with her about during the pregnancy was the baby's name. Once they found out it was a boy he had been rigid about naming the baby after him. Maxine loved the man but hated his name. There was no way under God's yellow sun she was naming anything popping out of her a Tally anything. His mother had picked that awfulness and as crazy as she was, Mother Emmerette Lancaster could keep it! Sounded too southern for someone like Tally himself and for sure her baby. Finally, they had settled on the name Tyson. Tyson Lancaster. He had been a funny looking newborn-- swishy little slanted eyes and large ears but by week three he had worn off the newborn newness and was as cute as ever.

Tally had been there for some of the midnight diaper change cries Maxine had been too sleepy to hear, he'd made sure their son was on time for the Sunday kids session at church and, with his mother and father's love and attention, Tyson was a fine young boy.

Like all parents facing situations such as these, Maxine wonders why on earth something like this had to happen. Tyson was such a high-spirited and fun kid. If she would have known being hit by a baseball could cause such a dire injury, she would have never let him play. Maxine had been leery of Tyson playing football for all of its unsafety but baseball, she thought, would have been harmless.

"Ma'am, I need to talk to you for a minute," the nurse snaps Maxine out of her thoughts. She pulls the curtain around the chair Maxine has just had her blood sampled at. "Your tests results show that you are A positive blood type. Your husband is also the A positive blood type. Tyson is B positive. Are you sure Mr. Lancaster is your son's father?"

"Wait--wait a minute? *What* did you just say to me? I *know* you are not trying to question my son's paternity? My husband is my son's father. End of story. And if you *ever question* me again, I'll—" Maxine is interrupted by the doctor.

"Elsie, it's fine. I'll take it from here," the doctor says to the nurse. The nurse walks away shaking her head and sighs. She's seen cases like this before.

The doctor pauses and looks Maxine in the face for almost a minute before speaking. "...Mrs. Lancaster...I know this is a touchy subject... But... We have to be clear here... We need to give Tyson a blood transfusion soon. He is losing blood. Your blood does not match. Your husband's blood type does not match. Is there possibly another person we could check for a match? I can guarantee you if we rely on a donor that'll take at least a day or so. I do realize this is a sensitive subject for you. We can try to keep the situation confidential. But honestly, time is of the essence, Mrs. Lancaster. The most important thing at the present time is stabilizing Tyson. The situation can be fixed. The longer we wait, the worse the situation for Tyson becomes. Okay. I'm going to give you a few minutes to think about this."

The doctor sounds grave. Maxine cannot utter a word. She feels like she is not really alive…as though she is sitting outside of herself watching herself and unable to help. When the doctor returns she still does not know what to say to him.

"…Well…Okay." He sounds awkward. "Mrs. Lancaster…what was your maiden name?"

"Irone…Irone—that's Iron with an e," she answers not knowing this is not one of the procedural questions the doctor needs to ask. "…My husband? Where is he?" She asks hoping Tally is not nearby.

"…He's in the waiting room now."

"What do you mean *now*?"

Totally ignoring the question the doctor continues, "Your first name is Maxine, correct?"

"…Yes." Maxine's stomach is now fizzling with discomfort. Something else is going wrong. She can feel it. "Something is wrong doctor—it's Dr. Vasil, right?"

Dr. Vasil gets straight to the point. "I think—well, no. I certainly do remember you. I have a photographic memory, you know." His voice is considerably lower than it was prior to now. He clears his throat. "You had a bachelorette party... I remember distinctly because there was a cake with your name written on it."

"Yeah...and?" Maxine vaguely remembers the cake Octavia had gotten with Maxine & Tally Lancaster Forever sprawled across it. She remembers cutting it and rubbing a piece all over the stripper before licking it off. "Look, my son is in this hospital and he's in the intensive care unit. Whatever you have to tell me about something nine years ago is irrelevant unless it has to do with this situation, no disrespect doctor."

"Okay." His voice is still curiously low. "Just a minute, Mam." He leaves the room and comes back seconds later. "Follow me please, Mam."

Maxine picks up her purse and follows the doctor to a room. He shuts the door. "Did you sleep with anyone other than your husband around the time you became pregnant with your son, Mrs. Lancaster?"

"Well—I—I did *not* and I do not appreciate you—"

"—I believe I was the dancer at your bachelorette party. I danced while I was in med school. I used to go by the name Black Adonis. I've long since shaved my head bald but...we—well, we spent some time together afterwards. Do you recall?"

Maxine says nothing.

"If you and I shared a night and it's slipped your memory, maybe you have conveniently forgotten another person as well?"

Maxine freezes her eyes on her shoes.

"Maybe you are still in contact with this person? If so, he can probably help."

"………………..There is no other person. Tally was my first. You—Black Adonis—WHOEVER THAT GUY WAS—THAT WAS THE ONLY OTHER PERSON I HAVE EVER SLEPT WITH… Honestly." Maxine knows the doctor has no reason to believe her but it is the truth. "…This is terrible…this is awkward as ever… But… Do you think you could see if your blood type matches my sons? …Please?"

"Mam…I am probably—definitely not your son's father. You need to figure out what you're going to do and go from there. If he needs a donor we will have to start that process," Dr. Vasil says obstinately. But honestly, he knows his blood type matches Tysons. Initially it seemed like a good idea to inform Maxine that he remembered her. He had been willing to donate his blood to the boy. Now, after some thought about the situation, he realized he was way in over his head and should have kept his mouth shut.

Had she come clean when he first asked her and stated that she had been with someone else, he would have donated and figured things out amongst his coworkers later. But she hadn't. So how was he to know whether or not she had slept with other men. That *could* be his son. The boy could also *not* be his son. He had let his and his husband Albert's desire to start a family consume him—to inhibit all common sense.

"Doctor—please! I would like to remain discreet about this. Tally has been there—Tally would be really hurt if he knew any of this. …Please… I—is there a way you can get a DNA test? Would you do that? If you were my son's father, would you donate blood to him?"

"That's if our blood types were to even match, Maxine--Mam. What I will certainly do is try to speed up this process so that he can get a transfusion by tomorrow night. Okay, Mrs. Lancaster?"

But something pulls on Antwan Vasil so hard he does secretly call for a DNA test. There is a nurse on the fourth floor that has owed him a favor after he caught her receiving oral from a Sickle Cell patient's father a month ago. They were going at it with the girl sleeping in the room. He text messages her to meet him in fifteen. An hour later the nurse covertly helps him administer a test. The next morning Antwan and Maxine are certain Antwan is Tyson Lancaster's father.

Can't Help Everyone

Ashley hadn't been nervous until now. She can't believe she let Lovey talk her into doing this. It's so stupid and weird. It's just what she gets for being too nice to people. Ashley doesn't even know this guy all that well. Since she'd started working at the health center the thirty-nine year old man been coming in everyday filling her time with heart-wrenching stories. She had agreed out of utter boredom. She has just moved to the small town. It hadn't been a month yet it seemed so much longer. She hadn't met anybody around her age to hangout with.

"We gon' git all of this and sue dis slum lord bastard, put it on da news, let people see how they got us livin'! Thanks fa comin. Go on and start it.'"

Ashley turns the camera on and captures the apartment building address. The building reminds Ashley of an oversized, crooked tree trunk; like the place was made out of a ragged treehouse. Something about the place gave her an off feeling. But lots of things in the town looked shanty and raggedy. And the entire town gave her an off feeling. Hopefully it wasn't too late to ask to transfer her internship to another town. First thing in the morning she'd have to call her sponsors and request to move.

When Lovey opens the door to the rather large unit she is instantaneously appalled. There are at least fourteen people in there—adults, kids and babies all over the place. It's messy and no one seems to care. An older lady with a smushed in nose, only her top dentures in with a scraggly scarf covering kinky gray hair and a worn-out housedress, bumps past them without saying a word to Lovey or Ashley. She is busy chewing on something unknown and disappears into the darkness of a room. Ashley is even more upset; with all the people in the place, surely one of them could have video taped this. *Why did he ask me to do this? This is just too weird! The number of people living in here is more disconcerting than the living conditions,* Ashley complains to herself.

"Let's git da kitchen! Look a-here! Da freezer ta da fridge ain't worked in uh year! ...You got dat? You got dat?" When he opened the freezer door a rotten fish smell took over the kitchen. "The paint is peelin,'" he added. "Look at da floor! Holes large enough to slide my foot in!"

He walks Ashley into three other rooms before he stops in a light green room with four mixed kids watching television as they sit at a round wooden table eating even though it is a bedroom and not a dining room or kitchen. Two of the kids with light brown, uncombed curls, cover their faces and act shy in front of the camera. His brother's Caucasian wife is in the room lying on a medical bed with a newborn baby on top of her chest.

Lovey snatches the baby from his younger brother's wife's arms and walks down the hallway. His sister-in-law is too weak to yell at Lovey and her husband is gone to work and not able to stand up to Lovey this time. "TAKE

DIS BABY TA DA HOSPITAL!" Lovey screams over and over. "TAKE HIM! TAKE HIM!" The infant begins to cry furiously. Lovey is holding him gawkily as he walks down the hallway and starts pressing into the infant's neck with the tips of his thumbs. "YOU SHOULDA WENT TA DA HOSPITAL!" he screams sticking his tongue out and pressing extra hard into the newborn. The baby's arm moves like a thunder lightning bolt before going limp and slowly descending next to the side of his small body.

Ashley looks at Lovey with the baby and backs out of the hallway. She cannot turn off the camera. Her fingers are too fidgety. She wants someone to call the police. Everyone around is attending to something else hidden in their rooms except for two older looking men Lovey had earlier introduced as his brothers who are playing guitars and singing a duet.

"YOU SET ME UP! YOU SET ME UP—YOU MADE ME DO THAT! YOU AIN'T NO GOOD! NONE UH Y'ALL AIN'T NO GOOD!" Lovey screams dropping the stiffness of the baby in a thud onto the floor but the pillow on the floor breaks the baby's fall. The baby is still alive. He slowly creeps toward Ashley trying to corner her. "Why you make me do bad things? *Whhhhhhy*?" he cries looking at Ashley with great aversion. There is nowhere for Ashley to go. She can't reach the front door of the apartment. He could easily angle her against the wall before she could make it to the door.

Ashley feels her bowels running down her pant leg. She hugs the camera, her head moving from side to side looking for an escape. She backs into the kitchen her foot sliding into a hole on the floor. She continues walking backwards until she leans against the metal bar of the outdated stove. If she can reach the pan hanging on the wall, maybe she can get him before he gets her.

Lovey, with one arm outreached, is still crying and ambling towards her in the kitchen. The camera is still rolling. Lovey's foot catches in a hole before he can reach Ashley's neck.

"…If the woman lied," one of Lovey's older brothers is singing still holding his guitar in front of him as he joins them in the kitchen. The other brother has a double barrel black and brown shotgun in his hand in place of his guitar. Both brothers continue singing their song as the one raises the gun a bit and squints his eyes. "Scoot back a lil honey," he says to Ashley in a soft, normal tone.

Just as she does the brother cocks his gun and Lovey falls backward. He opens his mouth and for a brief moment becomes a smiling caricature. His face contorts and twists until his tongue hangs out of his mouth as he clutches Ashley's ankle.

Ashley is immobilized. She feels an abhorrent energy transfer onto her ankle. The pulsation rises up to her calf and thru her entire body. Lovey sighs before his breathing is halted. Parts of his brain are splattered like dark red jam against the whiteness of the stove and Ashley's pant legs.

"Ya cain't mess wit, Lovey, chile. Dat boy been messin' with them drugs fa years—what got his brain so messed up," the brother issuing the bullet says to Ashley before turning back to his other brother and returning to their song. They both walk out of the kitchen back to where they were and began arguing about a chord in the song.

"**The FBI wants me!** They said if I get the witch out of me, they'll hire me. I've seen too many things. They know that. But I could be good on the team if we just work on that. I have a lot of hidden desires. I could really change my face and move to cities and work with the FBI. They know. They know everything. Last night they told me not to go to sleep. They told me you would over medicate me and kill me if I did. So that's why I don't go to sleep. And they wanting me to be drug-free when I come," Ashley inform the medical technician and nurse coming to give her a shot of Prolixin. Neither the nurse or the medical technician care. They've seen so many cases they can't anymore. The medical technician who is living well out of her means is currently worried about her car note. She's received two calls from the car company. The last time they called they threatened to garnish her wages. As far as the nurse is concerned this girl has a genetic mental illness just like the rest of them. "Let's just hope you can hold her down this time," the nurse says rather irritated to the medical technician who is in the beginning of a daydreaming about hitting the lottery and not having to worry about bill collectors ever again.

"No! None of that stuff!" Ashley shouts. "Didn't you just hear me? My soon-to-be husband is coming and he works for the FBI. He has been talking to me. He has ESP. He has extrasensory powers and he is sending me messages. If you give me that, I'll never be able to go with him. He told me—well—it's none of your business what he told me. You don't care about me. But he does. And I'll be working for the FBI. You won't. But I will be working for them."

On the psych floor there is Ezekiel who is addicted to and longing for his meds. There is Lucy who spreads her legs open in her hospital gown and constantly has one of the medical technicians on the psych floor staring at her coochie... There is Donald who thinks he can read minds... There is another girl who sees people no one else can see... There is another girl who was robbed yesterday and detoxing from heroine... There is Jerome who thinks he is Jesus and still not clean of cocaine... There is Bonnie who was slipped the date rape drug and at least ten more people in the psych ward going thru other similiar issues.

Ashley thinks one guy in there is in the FBI as well. She's caught him sending her messages over his coffee twice. Even with sleep aids at night the memories won't let her sleep. It always starts out the same. First there is Lovey asking her to help him and his family. Then there is the baby. Then the song, "...If The Woman Lied." Then there is Lovey giving her his polluted energy.

At first, after the police saw, they understood. But once she became psychotic and started hallucinating and became delusional she was put on Prolixin and was never able to properly explain the situation again. Ashley is here for a while before going to a group home.

The kids on the block call her The Crazy Girl and with her four braids standing on her head, and year round pastel gowns with boring triangles on them and all the talking to herself as she walks up and down the street who can blame them?

Other times, when she is under the influence of medicine, it is most difficult for Ashley to move without shaking.

She rocks back and forth in the motion of a cross. She thinks that by making a cross shape with her body she will eventually rid herself of the nightmares. The medicinal side affects cause her to become even more severely depressed, not be able to control her bladder and she is slowly developing a kidney problem.

Everyday she scrubs a ring around the ankle Lovey touched; the ankle is permanently raw.

Her parents are too embarrassed to bring her home. Even though they can be deadly, they would prefer she had cancer or lupus--anything but this type of psychotic diagnosis. They could have placed her in therapy. But after watching the video they just cannot understand how their daughter, working on a Master's in sociology could have gotten herself into such as situation with a person like that.

Like Garden Eyes

Adaptation 2

"You wanna drink?" Theena asks Daphnie leaving the pool to go to the bar in the basement of Daniel's house.

"Yeah, you know how us lushes do!" Daphnie replies concealing the fact that she is still leery of Theena calling and inviting her to come to town completely out of the blue.

Actually as lonely as Theena has become, she's been feeling secluded by force and starting to wonder if she had cut everyone from back in the day off too quickly. One thing Theena hated about herself was the fact that she never stood up for herself. With her, things were always one extreme or the other. In the past she either let a person walk all over her or cut them off. Surely there had to be a middle ground. Possibly she had been a little abrupt about things with Daphnie.

Kymberly is starting to act funny in Theena's opinion. She can't exactly explain it. She's just getting a funny vibe from Kym. She feels like she's always the first one to pick up the phone and call. Otherwise Kymberly doesn't call her. And the wives and girlfriends of Daniel's teammates have been shunning Theena since Theena's role in the play. She has constantly asked herself what could have possibly been so wrong with her role as a doctor in a play.

The now more than up-and-coming playwright Bristol had debuted his play in Atlanta and since the play had already received such rave reviews, it was scheduled to play on Broadway in the winter. Almost all the wives and girlfriends had come to Atlanta to see it. But they all started acting funny towards her when she told them she would be on Broadway and that she'd gotten excellent reviews as supporting actress. That she could almost handle but Candaleer and Kymberly giving her the cold shoulder was odd. Afterall, she had taken Candaleer to secretly see a fertility specialist against her husband's wishes and Theena had been there for two weeks when Kym had gotten her boob job.

Theena has told both of the girls way too much about herself. It hurts to think you're more of a friend to a person than they are to you.

"What would you like? We can make almost anything. Just look at all the liquor. Daniel has lots of parties here. Usually there's one like every Saturday when he's in town."

Daphnie feels like Theena is always bragging. "Umm..." Daphnie tries to think of something Theena might not know how to make so she can fix her own drink. When she and Theena were in the pool she caught Daniel looking at her butt. Before she even had a chance to think about it she had licked her lips at him. She hadn't thought Theena caught it but...had she? A few minutes after that Theena started talking about fixing her a drink. Theena *was* a bit vengeful. And what about when Daniel came in and surprised Theena? Theena had thought he was going out of town with his boys for two days. She seemed a little pissed he has come home with Daphnie there.

In Daphine's opinion, Theena has always been a bit insecure. Of course the little bitch didn't want her around with him there!

Theena checks a text message on her phone before turning her attention back to Daphinie. "What do you want? I'm fixing my own little special drink. It's Bailey's, vodka and two other things I can't tell you. It's my own little secret."

"I'll have the same thing. Just make mine strong." Daphnie laughs and walks to the other side of the bar next to Theena to watch her.

"Oh, nope! You can't see either!" Theena says totally oblivious of Daphnie's unfounded suspicions. Theena turns the other way as she pours the vodka. "You go over there, sit on the couch, relax and have a good time. That's what this weekend is all about."

"Yeah, I do need to unwind. I want to go to the mall and do some shopping a little later, though," Daphnie says not budging. *This chick is trying to do some shit to my ass. But that's cool. I'll pretend to drink it. And I'll make her take my ass shopping too. She got all those clothes and a closet the size of my bedroom. If I'm supposed to be her girl you'd think she woulda been offered to hook me up. If she can afford a Birkin bag, she can afford to look out for her girl,* Daphinie thinks ready to let the games begin. *Theena is kinda weak. I bet I can talk her into a threesome with Daniel if she gets enough drinks in her.*

"Here you go," Theena hands Daphinie a martini glass filled to the brim. "Let's make a toast. To bestfriends. We go way back, girl. We've been thru a lot together. We have our times when we don't always see eye to eye and I know I get on your nerves sometimes but I'm glad you're here. I feel bad we've been so distant lately."

They clank glasses.

Daphinie smiles.

I'm glad I ignored Daniel's texts. I can't believe him. My friend is not something in the rodent family! That's why I wish he would have gone out of town with Zabar like he was supposed to. I knew he was going to have a problem with Daphinie being here. Oh, well. She's not acting as funny as Kym and Candaleer and she's one of my best friends. He'll get over it, Theena thinks.

"Darling! I'm so proud of you!" Theena's mother exclaims upon reading the news that the play has received a Tony.

"Thanks mom! It's been hard work but *a lot of fun*," Theena responds walking to a newsstand to pick up a copy of The New York Times.

"Wait a minute mom. Daniel is on the other line. Hang on."

"What tha fuck is this?" Daniel shouts more than heated. "I just read that you tried to poison your best friend one night when she was at *my house*, that you secretly wanted a threesome with me and your best friend and that you got beat down by some girls back in Detroit! It's on all the gossips sites and all those shitty ass magazines at the grocery store. There's a whole article about you and me—

one night I couldn't get it up?! You *actually* told someone about that, Theena?"

The only person who knew about how her ex fiance had a crew of hoodrats beat her down was Daphnie. And Candaleer and Kym were the only two she'd ever told about Daniel's little impotence issue.

Like Garden Eyes

Dandelion Werewolf

Gordon Pierson can tell he is becoming more pronounced in years. He can't stand the loud, clancky chatter of all the young people on the train. Every so often they scream at something. They constantly flip thru each other's phone pictures. They scribble in magic marker on their canvas and cloth purses and book bags. And he finds their lip piercings and enlarged earring holes most alarming. One has the back of his neck pierced and his scroungy-looking, ratty girlfriend has the back of her wrist and both of her cheekbones pierced. Another one is wearing a mohawk that, at sixteen inches high, with feather-like curls shaped into its mold, looks more like a headdress. None of them are worthy of being collected. Then there is the Black woman with the convex chin and a salt and peppered ponytail holding onto the rail. She is coughing and spitting on the floor of the train. He wishes she would keel over and die.

      The dingy cream and brownness of the train displeases Gordon equally as much as the types the train contains. Most men of Wall Street in Gordon's position do not consider commuting by train. But there is a reason he has strategically parked his Benz in a parking structure for the day and has chosen this form of transportation.

He has seen her exiting the station four days consecutively. The elegant, elongated pale slender neck, the auburn billowy hair. Oh, yes. He had to see her in closer, enduring proximity this time. He scouted the station assiduously twenty good minutes or more but much to his chagrin had not found his beauty this fifth morning. Still, it is not a waste; more time to be meticulous about things. Until now he has not taken into consideration whether or not she will date a Black man. Other than the fact that she commutes by train, she looks well enough to do.

On second thought, Gordon decides this worry is a trifle. Types such as hers do not care about color. Color is the least of considerations with regards to things these days. Rather, the fixation revolves around economic status; a demarcation of the Haves versus the Have Nots.

What if she does not believe he is one of Wall Street's most reliable analysts? He cannot simply tell her information about himself on the train without looking pretentious. But how else will he be able to cozy up to her other than the train? He can try bumping into her near the newsstand and starting conversation. He has never resorted to public transportation—not even during undergrad at Columbia University. But no. No, he *had* to do it this way-- he had to take time to truly establish something.

The obsession with this woman continues well into the lunch at The Roll House with a few of his buddies from work. Barrone has interrupted him twice to ask how he is enjoying his raise. "It's great until the wife finds out. She'll increase the spending and it won't even feel as though I've received a raise." The other guys all laugh along with him.

As he sips his ale, his phone vibrates. "Hi honey," his wife says in her singsong voice.

"Hi, sweetheart. How's your day going?"

"Oh, gosh. I didn't realize until I got ready to go to lunch at Chanceux that I'd left my keys at home—the house keys. I separated my keys earlier by mistake rushing to get to the charity event and forgot them on the counter. Are you coming home after work or are you going to be in a meeting?"

'Meeting' had been Gordon's cover-up to Connie for the time spent at the Tribeca apartment. Now he'd have to forgo his evening plans. And what business did she have at Chanceux, so near his job?

"I'll skip out on the meeting—shouldn't be a problem, honey." He pretends to be unbothered. "We could have done lunch. Anyhow, what are you doing in my neck of the woods?"

"Well, a few of the ladies were a bit bored of the usual so they thought we'd give it a try. It would have been nice to have done lunch. You could have given me the keys so you wouldn't have to leave work early."

"No problem, sweetheart."

"Well you sound busy. I'll talk to you later, honey."

As soon as the conversation ends Gordon returns to his thoughts. Two months, maybe a few more and he'll have what he so longs for. Excitement. The sure. The unsure. A different experience even though he's had similar.

This has been much *easier than I thought. I'd expected more of a challenge with this one... Perhaps this is what should be* *expected of young ladies of her age these days,* Gordon thinks finding Susan's open friendliness towards him after only two weeks rather disgusting. *She doesn't interact this way with anyone else on the train, however*, he contests. He knows he has cantered into the situation in the precise manner and gained her trust. Even Connie teases he is a smooth talker.

"You know, it would be great if we could go for drinks tomorrow night," he says turning in his seat and looking into the beauty's green-flecked eyes right before their stop approaches.

"That—that sounds great," Susan responds.

"Well, I get off work a little late so how's eight? There's a great place in Tribeca I think you'd like… How about taking a cab? I'll pay for it."

"No. I can just meet you there. Where do you want to meet?"

Good, she doesn't want me to pick her up. Playing it cautious, aye? Gordon muses amusingly as he gives her directions to the bar on Chambers street. Underneath his placid and cool demeanor, he is enjoying the nervousness of it all.

The rest of the day goes by in a blur with Gordon doing just as he is expected at work. He has a way joking that makes his surrounding mix of uptight bosses and his hopeful, ladder-climbing inferiors at work a bit more lighthearted in the midst of the hectic velocity.

"Hi hon," Connie greets Gordon from the living room as he enters their Manhattan brownstone.

"Watch out for Chewy, you know how she gets when she's just had a bath dad," Gordon's son Irving warns rushing to hug his dad as he comes in from work. Chewy the Chihuahua rubs herself against Gordon's pant leg. He gives the dog a swift kick.

"Mommy said I can go camping tomorrow with Blair and Skyler if you say it's okay, dad," his ten year old daughter Elsie says running up for a hug as well.

"Sure, sweetheart," he responds. He turns to his wife. "The house looks great, how's the new help?"

"They're pretty good, I guess. No complaints so far." Connie kisses him on the cheek.

At night Connie is lying in bed watching *Law and Order*. It bothers Gordon that she is addicted to the show. "Turn that crap off. Every night you watch it twice."

"It's the only show I watch, honey," she cooes flipping the television off with the remote not upset she's missing the ending.

Gordon slides his hand against the softness of her nightgown.

"Turn the lamp off, honey," Connie requests. She never lets him make love with the lights on any longer since she's had the kids. Even with the tummy tucks and the breast lift she's still uncomfortable.

As they do the moves Gordon knows will not vary in routine, he lifts her silky hair and gently grazes her neck. He thinks of how simple it would be to break her neck. With one twist, he thinks he could get her. She's so fragile. Then she'll be gone. And he can move on. No, no. He'd never do anything to harm Connie. Her predictability is actually comforting to him. She is the one thing he can count on. As he rests his hand on her neck he is embarrassed of ever thinking of such a thing.

"What are all these paper clippings, honey? I'm trying to tidy up the boxes in the closet. I really prefer doing our bedroom and closet myself until I trust the new help, ya know. I found all of this." Connie thrusts a handful of newspapers articles at Gordon. "You hate *Law and Order* so, I don't see how you've saved up these. That Dandelion Werewolf or whatever they call him is just terrible." Connie shakes her head in disapproval. "It's his type that make me worry about the children whenever they aren't home."

Gordon takes the clippings and throws them into the bathroom wastebasket before kissing Connie and leaving for work.

"You're so funny." Susan places her hand on top of Gordon's. "And I love your name—Halloway Jaques. It has an indelible ring to it." She smiles at Gordon.

"Thanks. So how did you get into fashion merchandising?" Gordon asks pretending to care. Her college stories have been interesting enough but she is not as polished as he'd hoped and he finds the bright red lipstick staining her lips insulting to her face.

"Well, first, I wanted to be a clothing designer. I took a few classes at FIT and hated it. So then..." The rest floats pass Gordon as he motions the bartender for another round.

Gordon is at it again with Susan. This is the second time he has talked her into coming to his apartment.

"Halloway, dinner was wonderful," Susan says over the candlelights as she takes in the rooftop city view. "Handsome, funny and a great chef—I'm impressed." she adds.

"Shall we?" Gordon prompts her to dance.

"I have to warn you, I have two left feet." Susan giggles.

"Just follow my lead—you'll be fine."

On the second song Gordon wants to press his cheek against the gentleness of Susan's but doesn't. The feel of her fingertips against the chill of his knuckles gives him an erection. He pulls away so it will not be noticed. He guides her to the edge of the balcony.

"One day I hope to have a place like this," Susan says leaning over a bit.

Gordon goes to the table to pour her a glass of champagne then changes his mind. He goes back to where she is standing and leans in for a kiss. She closes her eyes and they kiss for a moment. "Open your eyes," Gordon commands. "I want to see you." Just as he says it, he pushes her off the balcony with all his might.

It is the look he expected, utter horror, fear, non-expectancy in her face--the exact thing he has been waiting and longing for. He savors the rush of redness to her cheeks now matching her lips. Her hands cocked over in an attempt to catch hold of the balcony—to break the twelve-story fall. He takes in his dangling's sweetness. The look in her eye pleads his help.

Instead he watches and smiles.

She should understand. It has to go this way. This way she will be immortalized. Her twenty-something beauty never to be altered by old age. This way he can collect all that she is at this very moment.

Nothing could be so sweet!

He leans over to watch, deliberately keeping his fingers away from the balcony. Her red dress descending from the sky faster than the flicker of the candlelight.

When his beauty descends, he does not waste any time. He blows out the candles and in one motion takes everything off the table by gathering up the tablecloth and heads back into his apartment without bumping into anyone. Gordon learned from the talkative doorman two days ago that there had been an outage with the cameras in the building that still has not been fixed.

Gordon lights a cigar replaying the day he first met her to the minutes ago they last kissed.

This is better than the time he caught a pigeon in the backyard of his house when he was a young boy. He stepped on its wing and trapped it before burning the pigeon to a stinking, feathered tar. When his dad had come outside and witnessed what he'd done he'd said, "Filthy shits. That's what they deserve. I hate pigeons." But his mother had taken a different approach to other such happenings and had tried to douse him in guilt. "Gordy," she'd say, "Your brothers are not like you—I expect different of you. You are not that type of boy, Gordy.

You're sweet and obedient and kind. Stop it with the rough-housing and animal incidents already!"

And in grade school it had been the same. A whole school year of good behavior unmarred by one insignificant trifle or two. He'd cut Cindy Ludemire on the arm in the fifth grade with a box cuter and, deemed a mistake by Cindy and the art teacher, ran scott-free.

This was different. There was no one to brush over things and make excuses. He had done this, short and simple. This had been his month's great toil. As annoying as her voice could sometimes become, she was his angel. She'd appreciate him for this as she looked down upon him soon. There was no greater feeling than being someone's savior.

He walked into the bathroom, locked the door and flushed the clippings he'd retrieved from the wastebasket days ago down the toilet. The Dandelion Werewolf had collected five of them now. Lola Sayers, Eva Robertson, Danny Ferns, Orchid Cattaraugus and Susan Peterson. Each one had held the same look of weak helplessness in their last moments. This last one would be no different. He would sublease this apartment just like the last four apartments for a bit higher than he'd paid. The alibi was certainly in place. He'd been home, in the basement listening to his favorite records. No one had seen him leave. Besides, he very well held no implications, as far as he was concerned.

He takes the freight elevator in the back of the building before melting into the crowd in the lobby. He tilts his hat lower and rubs his face to ensure his prosthetic nose is still in place and slides out of the first floor's back entrance. He desperately desires to be an onlooker but realizes how truly unrealistic that is now. Police cars encircle Susan's body.

There'll be no more. *Not for some years. Most only get caught out of greed. This is enough for now.* Gordon, fully loaded on content, carefully rolls into bed next to a peacefully resting Connie.

No Other—A Tribute For The One

She sits on the corner of her antique, thrift store bed listening to UK neo soul while thinking about him...

The minute she got off the bus, out of the blue, he rushed out of his seat in the St. Louis Greyhound station to help her with her things, meanwhile, her extremely bucked toothed boyfriend who had been creeping out all the other people on the bus ride rushed away to charge his phone leaving her with all the luggage. How he had even spotted her so fast was a mystery--one of those things men do after spotting unmatched beauty.

He wasn't real tall or short, maybe 5' 9, shoulder length neat dredlocks, slim, carmel skinned with a St. Louis drawl. He stayed seated behind her hoping she would hear him talking about how perfect she was to the guy next to him once they got back on the bus.

She'd managed to slip him her business card during a stop in Kansas but had to play it off and gave it to a few others so Bucktooth wouldn't be alarmed. Actually, she didn't want him to think ill of her for being with Bucktooth and coming at him. And she didn't want to insult Bucktooth since he had come along across country to accompany her while she worked so she wouldn't be alone.

At the station in Kansas he sat near her and Bucktooth and smiled at her at during the stop while trying to guess her and Bucktooth's connection. But she didn't know he was watching her like that. It wasn't until days later, after going over the entire situation in her mind that she figured it all out.

Though he said nothing, once in Vegas he had followed her outside since Bucktooth had remained inside the Vegas station watching the Wendy Williams show. On the way to Cali he sat near the tiny bus restroom all alone on the last row of seats half asleep, half dreaming of what she tasted like.

When she got up to use the restroom she tried not to stop and stare at him. The short time she used the restroom she tried to figure out a way to sit next to him instead of her bucktoothed, supposed to be boyfriend or how to at least slip the dude her number since it wasn't on her card.

In Utah when they stopped in the mountains, she couldn't find him after she got off the bus. Bucktooth stayed on the bus and away from her, which was a good thing. It would have been the perfect chance to say something. But instead, the undercover bus security guy kept talking and talking to her outside the convenience store about wanting a different girl even though he was with his kids' mother. She didn't realize what he was up to until later. Once back on the bus, the undercover security guy sat next to her dream dude and told him to go up to her and say something even though she was with Bucktooth. The security dude told her dream guy that she wasn't happy with Bucktooth; he could tell. And how right he was. And how horrible it was hearing her dream dude talk about her without being able to do anything. He said he was worried she had kids with Bucktooth. He couldn't bare that, he said. He had even looked up her website from the info on her card on his phone.

She smiled although a tear fell down her left cheek as he went on and on about how perfect she was. From the way she talked to the way she moved her hands, even her edgy, bright hair—he said he liked it. Hardly anyone got her hair. But he did.

Later, as they drove around miles and miles of brown dusty mountains and rocks, a not so cute, bony, dark skinned guy in glasses seated next to her dream dude deterred him from saying something since she was with the bucktoothed boy. The dark skinned guy had said, "Man, she's not worth it if she's with *that* dude!"

What a mistake keeping that bucktoothed creep! A liar of more than ten months! Had gotten up every day and casually dressed up supposedly for work but as it turned out when she went to visit where he worked, they had never heard of dude. With no job, no education, not even good looks to keep things going...only grape sized balls and bad breath, he had been a total waste of time! Money can be attained back with time. But time can never be gotten back once wasted.

She knows she should have said something to the dude with the locks.

Thoughts of him forever play in her mind over and over, relentlessly like a favorite song scratched. What it would be like to touch his face, his smile...how electric it would be to hold his hand. She could see herself doing things she never dreamed of doing for any other man, just for him. Nothing would have mattered with him.

It is a longing that sits in between the curves of the mind and tortures as it delights, missing this guy. This man. He was definitely younger than her, although no one except she could tell. She was something back then, two years ago. Much has changed lately thanks to depression's timeless lingering bells of destruction.

Being with the wrong person, being in the wrong place can do that to the soul. No one understands. They all think she should be happy. But she hasn't really been in a upbeat mood since bumping into that one guy in St. Louis. She had a bounce back then--a style. Not just in the jagged, skinny blonde locks. It was more than that. It was confidence and contentment.

Some say there is only lust at first site. But she knows this is incorrect; when you know what you know, no one can tell you different. There is such a thing as knowing from the initial moment. It happened to her once before. In the sixth grade. Martin Calberry. He was the new boy at school. The day they introduced him to the class, though those short red shorts of his didn't collide well with his tall stature, she knew he was going to be her boyfriend. And once they did find themselves in puppy love, it was all the rage. The first love she ever had. One of the very best.

All of this only confirms for her that that St. Louis boy was The One. Even after dumping Bucktooth and trading him for a smolderingly fine, dark skinned dude with an intriguingly strong spiritual bent, there was an emptiness. A longing for the lockhead.

It will be tough for another to touch this sort of thing.

The thing is, she does not know that she, too, taunts the lockhead's memories. Bucktooth once told her the night before she kicked him out of her life forever that the lockhead still thought of her. That is the only fond memory of Bucktooth she has. Even though he bought her a puppy, even though Bucktooth paid for that one trip to Cali, none of that counts.

His exact words were, "The way that guy talked about you for hours on the bus, he still thinks of you from time to time, trust me." And for that and only that, she appreciates Bucktooth. She does not know that he is in fact correct. She also does not know that the lockhead never guessed she liked him and wanted him with the same amount of fervor. He will never know…unless he reads this.

There are a few other guys (including Bucktooth) who still think of her and the way she smells of that one Bath and Bodyworks purple body spray and of the way she knows precisely how to spoil a man. But none of those guys matter now. Only The One matters. The dream she met in the flesh if for only a few moments in time.

Like Garden Eyes

Sacrifice

"**Excuse me, where are** the books on genetics located?" Fanny Hammond asks the librarian for the fifth time. The librarian is not a fan of Black people and takes great pleasure in ignoring Fanny. This is not the first time and won't be the last. It's like a routine game they play. Fanny, a graduate student in her third year, is used to this. Usually Fanny struggles thru the library catalogs or asks someone white to ask the librarian a question for her when she can't locate the information she needs on her own. It's the late seventies and, even with all the last decade's civil rights marches and leaders who have died for a cause, people in this area like to wear their disdain for "The Blacks" proudly on their shoulders.

    Weary and tired from fighting to stay positive after receiving a C on a paper in a philosophy class from an instructor who is as discriminatory as the librarian, Fanny doesn't feel like fighting today. Instead she plops down in one of the wooden chairs at the long center table and allows herself to sulk for a few minutes. *I helped Laurie Ann with her paper and she gets and A+, meanwhile, I receive a C! I worked on that paper for weeks*, she laments to herself.

There is a group of Black kids gathered at the end of the long table where Fanny sits.

"Hush up! You guys always come in here with all that ruckus! Don't see why ya reading anyhow! Ain't gone be nothing but a buncha maids and bums someday!" a white security guard barks at the kids. They all stop giggling to look up at him.

Without thinking Fanny jumps up out of her chair and marches over to the kids. "Listen. I wanna tell you all, YOU ALL! You can be anything you want to be. And you can be something.

"You can be a doctor!" She points at a young boy in a yellow torn tee shirt. "You can be a lawyer!" She points at the girl in two tiny ponytails. "All of you will be something—not no maids and not no bums!" Two of the kids look up at Fanny and smile. A few others look down not knowing what to say. A shy brown skinned woman wearing the same cream lace top underneath a velvet dress she wears everyday seated at the table behind all the children turns around and looks at Fanny for a while. She parts her lips to say something but does not know what to say. "Honey, don't let nobody talk to your kids that way! These kids are gone be something one day!"

The lady has seen how the librarians treat Fanny on more than one occasion. She knows enough to know that Fanny has never taken up for herself. She wants to tell Fanny thank you but feels embarrassed for reasons she herself does not understand. Really Francis, the mother of these nine children, is used to bad treatment. At the doctor's office the doctors ridicule her for having so many kids. They beg her to get on birth control and to think of giving some of her children up for adoption. Two doctors have gone so far as to call her stupid. Her welfare worker is a Black lady but she is just as bad. She refers to Francis' children as her litter instead her children and threatens to take Francis off welfare unless she gets sterilized.

Francis figures it's just the way life goes. Born down south in Mississippi Francis had only gone up to sixth grade before having to join her parents in the cotton fields. She'd met a man who offered to take her off her parents' hands and they'd been more than happy at his offer but after baby number seven he walked off. Another guy came along and married her even with all the kids and moved her to Michigan but after the ninth child never returned home. He hadn't even come to the hospital for the last child's birth.

But the kids had made things worthwhile. Francis had finally found love in each and every one of them. And although they stayed in a two-bedroom place in the projects, Francis finally had laugher in her home. It might not have been much but she finally had a home worth going to.

"I'm Francis," she finally said and put her hand out to shake Fanny's.

From that the friendship begins. Everyday at five o'clock the two women meet up and share their daily trials and tribulations. Francis usually brings Fanny a sandwich in exchange for the reading lessons Fanny gives her and all the homework help Fanny doles out to the kids. Neither Francis nor Fanny have had a friend in years. For Fanny, being the only Black woman in the English Ph.D. program, she's found the only way to get by is by being helpful to her study groups. But it usually doesn't last. They usually always find a way to exclude her unless she helps them with their assignments. Even with that, Fanny knows soon, as always, they will find a way not to need her.

For Francis, even within the projects she is considered a miser. She doesn't dress in the fashionable bell-bottoms and doesn't press her hair or polish her nails like the other women in her neighborhood. No matter the season she wears her one, velvet dress and hides her nappy plaits in a velvet tam.

Fanny, with her extra, extra broad nose and unstraightened hair has known exclusion as well. Every semester she is begged to quit the program and find a more suitable career. Nurse, teacher, why-o-why can't she be more reasonable! What good would a Ph.D. do a woman such as herself the school dean had implored her!

To the library regulars watching, the two ladies over the span of two years have become peculiarly close. Whispers of funny business have even started. What people don't realize is that sanity is always underrated. Day to day survival may not have occurred for either one of these ladies had their stumbled upon friendship not arisen.

It is just another dreary day in town. Here even the sunny days look gloomy and unpromising. Today Fanny and Francis have met up outside at the picnic table next to the lake across from the library.

There is a Black guy sitting at the picnic table behind theirs. His medium length hair is wild and fights the wind. His baggy clothes are tanned with dust. He is spread out across the bench of the picnic table.

There is something about his eyes that bother Francis. They look more like two bullets instead of pupils. And his eyes seem to move away from each other rather than in unison as most human's do. For a few seconds it looks to Francis like the man is completely missing eyeballs.

"You homeless!" the bum shouts at Fanny.

"No, *you're* homeless!" Fanny shouts back at him. "Ya bum!" she adds.

"Sssh. Don't say nothing to him." Francis says to Fanny. "Let's go inside. That man don't look right," Francis adds grabbing her purse and Fanny's book bag.

The next day Francis slides her purse on the table and sits on the picnic bench to wait for Fanny. The weather is too nice to be inside. A few minutes later the bum is back. Francis' back is turned so she has no way of knowing until it is too late. The bum is seething. He has stayed up all night in the park down the street plotting and planning.

He slides his swollen, weathered hands around Francis' neck. "Where she at? WHERE SHE AT?" he demands. Francis says nothing while struggling to free herself from his grip. "WHERE?"

He drags Francis to the lake and tumbles in, repeatedly screaming for Fanny. The few people down the street run into the library for cover. Someone tells the security guard who calls the police. "TELL ME AND I'LL LETCHU GO! TELL ME! WHERE SHE AT?"

Francis never responds. He gets tired of Francis' non talking shenanigans and pulls out a knife he had sharpened the night before and repeatedly jabs Francis in the jugular vein of her neck until he is content and Francis no longer struggles.

Francis could have told him Fanny would be in the library soon. She could have told him.

Everyone in the library is in fear. Efforts have been made to lock all doors until the police arrive. Fanny arrives right after the police reach the scene.

To the judicial system, Francis was just another welfare mother who wasn't doing anything with herself. Her killer has long since been diagnosed with a mental illness. Medical records proved that his condition seemed to worsen once medicated; something about unusual behavior, intrusive and inappropriate thoughts linked to side effects. And after all, he has killed one of his own--no big deal. They give him five years and then he is set free. Fanny's appeals mean nothing. No one else appeals the case. Other than a small article written from a neutral viewpoint, no fuss has been made by anyone other than Fanny, for that matter.

Fanny has managed to purchase a four-bedroom home for Francis' kids and herself. It was a fight to prove she could manage all the kids but, in the end, the system had nowhere else to place nine brothers and sisters even if they were to separate them. And somehow—even with all the kids—Fanny has managed to finish school.

But she had no idea that when the man was released from prison he was moved to a half way house on the

Boulevard within blocks from her home in the McGraw area. He has thought about her and even thought about pursuing his hunt for her but will eventually become obsessed with something else.

One day unknowingly Dr. Hammond will walk right by the heavily supervised group home Francis' killer now resides involuntarily after being quote unquote rehabilitated. He will be sitting on the porch but, eyes and mind zoned out from his meds, he will not recognize her.

Like Garden Eyes

It Doesn't Always End The Way It Starts

"**Hey, Lim! Whassup, whassup!**" a woman in a man's oversized tan Carhart jacket, baggy cargo overalls and ran over looking tan boots exclaims.

Limner Peale cannot place just who the woman with pores large enough to stick a number two pencil eraser in, with no more than five rotten teeth remaining, wearing a paisley scarf and black scull cap slung on top of her head now overly smiling at him is.

"Awww, don't try to play nobody like you 'on't know 'em nah, Limner Peale."

Still he cannot tell who this person is. Nothing about her is familiar. In fact he thought she was about to ask him for a dollar. Bums at this particular gas station are rather brazen these days. They ask, or suffice it to say, demand, a couple of dollars from anyone including children. He is only in town to visit his parents and glad he moved from the area decades ago.

Finally, the woman puts her hand on her hip and leans to the side and says her name with a teasing attitude, "Calla*hond*ria Jackson."

Before he can prepare for it, his one-time high school love of one year grabs and hugs him. The only thing he can think of for a few seconds is going home and showering in very, very hot water for a good twenty minutes.

Callahondria Jackson. Once Murray Wright's, prettiest face, the favorite clarinet girl. Now this.

"So what are you doing with yourself these days?" Limner asks stepping back so as to avoid her breath from reaching him.

"*Boy*!" She taps him on his arm playfully. "I'm uh nurses aid fa Ascension's nursing home. Yep, yep. An' you still lookin' good. I likes dat shiny brand new Cadillac sitting over dere!" She laughs in smoker's cough fashion and slightly hunches over as she picks up her change from the cashier for her loose smoke.

"Yeah…yeah, thanks." If anyone worth mentioning was in the gas station Limner would have taken off and ran from the embarrassment of someone like this knowing him. "Great seeing you," he lies. "Thirty on seven," he adds to the cashier and walks back to his car. As he pumps the gas he shakes his head reminiscing about how Callahondria used to dog him out and berate at him in front of the other marching band members and how he took it because he felt special being with the one and only CC Jackson. She was so popular. Even though she thought he was a Pointdexter and a yuppie because he was smart and wasn't cool, she'd gone steady with him because of where he lived and because everyone thought he had money since his father had been the school principal.

Limner had bought Callahondria a promise ring once that she gave away. She had demanded he buy her a bigger one within a week. Funny thing was, he did end up saving up and buying her another diamond ring along with a pendant necklace and she was still pissed because it had taken him a month instead of a week like she told him.

He spent the entire summer before going to Harvard arguing with her and trying to get some whenever she wasn't mad at him—which was rare. She had been accepted to Marygrove and was supposed to go there fall of 1986.

Like Garden Eyes

Shamar & His Wife

"**Hi honey. I'm at Meijer.** I'm making chicken cacciatore and string bean casserole, kung pao chicken, baking some salmon, rice and salad, meatloaf and mash potatoes. I need like two more meals for the week. Anything special you want?" Cilana asks holding her phone against her left shoulder and ear while getting the baby and Shamar Junior out of the Lexus Truck and into the grocery cart.

"Honey, I'm kind of busy right now. There's a lot going on in the office today. Sounds good so far—just pick something, okay?"

"Well, okay," Cilana responds thinking, *don't complain next week that I didn't cook anything you liked.* "Well, hope everything at work goes okay. Love you, honey. Bye."

"Bye," Shamar rushes off the phone. He's not really all that busy. Actually, he's having a slightly bad day. He just got what he considers to be a less than appealing quarterly review—seven and a half points out of ten. He is always on time, picks up extra work, goes to industry workshops and conferences in order to keep abreast of the field and doesn't join in the break room complaining sessions or ask for any on the job comforts. Part of him feels it's because he is the only Black in the office. He feels he deserves an eleven out of ten but ten points would have sufficed. What tha fuck was a seven point five? They could have kept the point five! Or at least made it an eight. Then the dealership called and said Cilana's truck was over mileage. Twenty-one was too young to have gotten married. He should have attained his master's degree first. That probably would have made him even more of a candidate for supervisory positions. But everyone at the kingdom hall had warned him that the system was ending soon. "There was no point in storing up treasures in this world. He *already* had a bachelor's degree." They had constantly reminded him.

And just getting that bachelors degree had been a big deal. When he got accepted to Howard on full scholarship his parents had had such a conniption, he only managed to stay one semester. But leaving hadn't been that bad. He'd had a good time at Oakland University, finished early and had a position as a ministerial servant at the kingdom hall.

Now Cilana was a different story. All the brothers at the hall had their eyes on her even now. She was classy, came from a good, theocratic upbringing, very feminine and tried to please him. But his family had been shocked he married a Black girl. The entire year they dated his parents thought it was just a phase.

Secretly he is starting to feel a little suspicious of the whole thing. When they dated, everything had gone well--almost too well. He couldn't see it back then. He thought they were going to date two years and be engaged another year. But, Cilana, sweet, darling Ms. Cilana, had read some book by some relationship guru and had clobbered him with an ultimatum. "It had been six months and she needed to be reassured they were headed somewhere," she'd said. He hadn't responded. The next time he called she casually announced that she was about to go out on a date with a brother from the congregation that met across the hall from his. He had gotten so upset he ended up taking her to look for a ring the next week. Everything had been pretty good after that until Cilana got pregnant with Shamar Junior on the honeymoon.

At the time, he hadn't been too concerned. Doing all the things they did those five nights in Trinidad definitely made that a possibility. But right after that, not even a full three months later she had gotten pregnant again with Cilan. That put pressure on him. He had always wanted to be an excellent provider. He couldn't see staying in an apartment with two kids. He had a reputation; he was a Strother. So, with his parent's help, he'd purchased a house in Macomb Township. Four-hundred thousand dollars of a house. And granted, he made good money—eighty thousand dollars a year—but things were just going too fast; there were lots of obligations.

Almost twenty-four, he shouldn't be feeling like life is this heavy.

Junior, at a year and a half, is being very uncooperative with Cilana right now. "You have to stay in the shopping cart, JR!" Cilana sighs as she crosses the crosswalk and enters Meijer. If only Shamar could see this right now. JR acts like a little angel whenever Shamar's around. Shamar doesn't seem to think two kids—a one and a half year old and a four-month infant--are as much work as they are. But what's bothering her even more than that is the way Shamar has been acting for the last two months. Oh, sure. She's still been her bubbly self. She's been calm about things waiting to see if Shamar will bring up what's been troubling him lately. Problem is he hasn't. He's becoming more and more aloof, easily agitated and gruff. Cilana hopes it's nothing major going on with him. She doesn't think he's cheating or anything like that. Actually, truthfully, she is starting to think plain and simply it's that she gets on his nerves. She's not as dumb as most people think. She can tell people think she's not exactly bright on the intelligence end. It's the way they talk to her or try to make comments that they think will go over her head. Sometimes she plays along with the whole dimwit shenanigans, other times she really doesn't care. It just depends on who's doing it.

The more she thinks about it, Shamar *is* probably starting to get bored with her and he certainly thinks she's dumb. The other day he was watching the world news and yelling at the television regarding some issue with the war in Iraq. When she entered the room he tried to explain it to her but she didn't really care. Cilana has never been into fighting or politics. *Maybe I should watch CNN sometimes...maybe that will help.* Seconds later Cilana laughs at the thought. Unless it's the Sunday coupon section, she couldn't care less about the world news or any other kind of news. Intelligence is subjective, Cilana thinks. *Just because I don't have a degree doesn't mean I'm stupid. I am smart in the subjects I care about.*

"Hi Cilana," Jeannie Albright says catching Cilana between the strawberries and plums. JR is grabbing at the container of strawberries in Cilana's hand. She moves them out of his reach right before he has a chance to knock over the plastic container. "How are things going?" Jeannie asks before directing her attention to JR. She coos at him for a couple of seconds. "Can I pick him up?" she asks.

"Sure," Cilana responds.

"Why don't you bring the kids over tomorrow in the afternoon for a little playtime. My grandkids are going to be over." Jeannie suggest to Cilana's delight. The fifty-something Caucasian lady's husband is the coordinating elder at their congregation. *And to think I almost thought she didn't like me. If she's inviting the kids over, surely she likes us. Wait until I tell Mari about this.* He was already a servant but it would be really nice if Shamar became an elder in the near future. That would really impress her parents. That would impress everyone—especially as young as they were. They'd be setting a good example in the congregation. And Jeannie's husband is just the one who could make Mari an elder. "Is it okay if he sits here?" Jeannie asks pointing to the front seat of her shopping cart.

"Sure." Starting to feel more comfortable with Jeannie, Cilana tells her of her latest dinner predicament as they shop together. "Any suggestions of what to fix? I need two more meals."

"Wow. I'm impressed. You know how to cook lots of different meals.

Jeannie saying that really makes Cilana feel good. She tries so hard to be a good wife, a good daughter, a good friend but not too many seem to notice.

"Yeah, I go online and get different recipes and test them out and I take cooking classes at Macomb Community College Continuing Ed. I love to cook."

"I'm sure you'll figure out something good to fix. Why not fix Shamar's favorite meals? You can't go wrong with that. ...You're good at a lot of things, honey. I heard from Naomi how nicely you decorated your house."

Not wanting to look overly happy, Cilana swallows a smile. That was nice to hear as well. Naomi had come over to one of the 'Sisters Night Out' she hosted at her house. Usually Naomi acted like she didn't really care for Cilana. Cilana had chalked that up to the fact that Naomi was still looking for a husband and unattractive and a little rough around the edges.

"You've had us over a lot. You *have* to come over." Cilana is feeling terrible she never invited Sister Albright over and wondering how she could have forgotten her when she had the housewarming. She ended up having almost two hundred people over and the day of the party she and Shamar were arguing over how many people she had invited. Other than the argument the entire party was a blur.

"You all are in that new sub-division off Twenty-Four Mile, right? The gated one?"

"Yeah."

"Shamar let us walk thru it when they were almost done building it but, no, I haven't seen it since you all moved in."

"Hi, honey. Dinner's on the table waiting for you," Cilana informs Shamar greeting him the minute he comes in from work and takes his shoes off. "Guess what? I bumped into Sister Albright at Meijers and she invited the kids over tomorrow."

"That's cool. I like the Albrights." Next to the prayer before dinner, that is the only thing Shamar says during the entire meal.

Cilana is trying not to frown and keeps looking up from her plate at Shamar. *I probably have no right to be mad. He is just being a guy and doesn't feel like talking. He said he had a busy day. He's just tired. ...It's just that I hardly get any adult conversation all day... It would be nice if he at least asked me how my day was. He is so cute, he's good to me but he just acts so funny lately! I need to go online tomorrow and look up an article on how to repair communication. This is not good.*

Cilana is upstairs in the den doing Zumba while Shamar watches Sportscenter on the flat screen in the basement. Even her doing Zumba everyday is getting on his nerves. He knows he should be happy she stays fit and feels guilty for being irritated by her. When she's done unless one of the kids wakes up, she's going to come downstairs and try to talk him into going to bed early so they can do it.

Sure enough, forty-four minutes later Cilana comes downstairs wearing a turquoise ruffled bra and panty set. "Mari, do you feel like coming to bed?"

"What? No, not really... Your sister called. Why don't you call her back?" Shamar brushes her off. It's his wind-down time. She should know that by now. Besides, if he goes upstairs, with the way things have been going, they'll probably end up with babies number three, four and five. Triplets. Cilana is a Fertile Myrtle. Just the thought of more kids wilts his dick. Don't get it wrong; he loves his son and daughter. But they do cost money and they take a lot of time.

"Lana, get the phone!" Shamar yells from the basement after answering the house phone.

"Who is it?" she asks still smarting from his chilly reception.

"Danita!"

Cilana picks up the phone in the bedroom and lies across the bed. She wants to tell Danita about this thing with Shamar but she doesn't know if that's a good idea. They don't really have that kind of relationship with each other. Cilana gets the feeling Danita is only around because they are one of the only other young Black couples in the congregation and because of their reputation. "Hello?"

"Hey, Lana. Whassup? We're going to CJ Barrymore's Sunday after the meeting. You and Shamar are welcomed to come."

"Okay, I have to see what he says. I'll let you know tomorrow for sure."

"Girl! Your suit last night was sharp. Where'd you get it from?"

Danita was talking about the suit Shamar had gotten from a boutique in Beverly Hills when they went out of town last month for his job. "I'm not sure. Mari picked it up somewhere in LA last month."

"How much was it?" Danita asks unabashedly.

"...I'm not sure," she answers regarding the four-hundred dollar suit that was clearanced at eighty. Cilana is a shop-a-holic but she definitely only revels in sales. Amongst the many things her mother had taught Cilana and her sisters such as 'never deny your husband sex for any reason whatsoever,' her mother had also taught them not to ever buy anything *not* on sale. "Hey, thanks for calling, girl but I have to go. Shamar is calling me," she lies. It was time to get off the phone before anymore inquisitions started. The last time Danita called she wanted to know how much of Cilana's hair was real which had totally pissed Cilana off. Danita who would wear a short wig to the hall followed the next week by one as long as Cher in the seventies, didn't seem to care about tackiness. Cilana's hair is long but lately she'd been wearing a few tracks to make it a little more exotic. Shamar would kill her if he knew. He hated anything fake including nails, which was why she had gel overlays on her own instead of tips.

Cilana is feeling terribly lonely. She wants to go check on the kids in their bedrooms but fears one of them waking up and because of that doesn't. The baby monitors are on and both sound fine.

She decided to turn on the iPad Mari had just bought her and logs in to her Facebook and Twitter accounts. On Facebook she has three hundred friends most of whom are Jehovah Witnesses. She checks the five new messages she has and gets a few good laughs from friends across the States. She leaves a couple of messages on the walls of a few of her friends from Ontario. *Everything is great she says in her status bar. Taking some ballroom classes with Mari next week*. On Twitter she has a few new followers. It's now an hour later and Shamar has still not made any advances to the bedroom.

She picks up her phone and calls her younger sister Celina.

"Hey, Lana."

"Hey. Mari is pissing me off! He is acting so strange lately, Lina."

"Girl—whatever. He's a guy. That's how they all are. Tim hasn't even called me all day and he still hasn't gotten fitted for his tux." Celina is about to be married four months from now and that is the only thing the entire family has been talking about.

"You know what, Lana—let me call you back. This is him on the other line."

"Okay. Bye."

Cilana calls her mother. "Hi, mommy. I am totally pissed. Mari is acting funny lately. Hardly talks to me…I don't know what's going on with him, ya know?"

"Yeah, well, sweetie, Mari is a good guy. Give him a break. He works hard and has a lot going on at the hall. Someone was just telling me how good his talk was last night's meeting."

"…Yeah. Well…Sister Jeannie Albright invited the kids over tomorrow."

"Oh, really? I like the Albrights. That sounds nice—you know what? I had better get off here. I almost forgot. I have to call and make sure your sisters have all gotten fitted for Lina's wedding. I promised that girl I would check. I was supposed to call them yesterday. Goodness gracious. Okay, Lana. Have a good night. Call me tomorrow. And remember, give Mari a break. He works hard to provide for you and the family and he's a good guy. Pray to Jehovah about it and make sure you're doing everything on your end a wife is supposed to be doing. You're me and your dad's daughter but we have to stay out of your marriage. They just had an article last month in the *Awake!* about that. Parents have to stay out of their children's marriages! I've got five daughters and my baby Lina is the last to get married. All of you all are going to be gone now. Don't come to me with all that arguing stuff. Okay, bye, sweetie." Click.

Cilana rolls over onto her pillow and breaks into an uncontrollable sob fest. She tries to silence her cries with the pillow. Nothing seems right. Almost twenty-three she shouldn't be feeling like this—she's got all the things she's ever wanted. No one should feel so lonely. She feels like a remote arid, desert no one will ever visit. After crying until she can't any longer, she rinses her face, wraps her hair for the night and goes to bed.

Shamar is flipping thru channels and stops briefly on Destiny's Child "Cater to You" video. He flips it off because it reminds him of Cilana. She is *always* trying to attend to his every need. Sometimes it becomes asphyxiating and highly annoying. It would be nice if she fought back a little bit every now then—if there was a bit of fire underneath all the benevolence. On second thought, he thinks it's probably better that she doesn't. The way things are right now, she respects him as the head of the house and pretty much does what he tells her. As she should. He takes good care of her. There's nothing she wants that she doesn't get. All she has to do is putter around the house and do her girly stuff. Tomorrow he's going to tell her to shut down her Facebook and Twitter sites. Every time he watches the news they have more warnings about that crap. And he's going to have to talk her into getting better birth control.

His homeboy Wallace from back in the day is calling. Even though it's late Shamar answers his phone. "Whassup, man?"

"Man, Alicia just put me out. We got into it and it got real crazy. I wanted to *sock the mess* out of her, man. She came across my porn collection and now she wants to tell the elders. You better be glad man. You got a good one, man. At least your wife doesn't try to throw hot water on you!"

"Yeah, man, Lana's alright. Sometimes she gets on my nerves, but nah, she'd never do crazy stuff like *that*."

"You think I can crash at your place for a week or two, man?" Wallace asks.

"…Man… We've got a lot going on. The kids are always crying and keeping my wife busy…" Shamar shuts his boy down. After eight-thirty the kids are usually knocked out—Cilana has them on a schedule. Cilan might wake up in the middle of the night usually only once or twice but Cilana usually catches that before the baby has a chance to wake him.

It's just that Wallace can't crash at his house. First of all Wallace is not doing all that great spiritually in the congregation. It wouldn't be a good look to have him hanging around his family. Secondly, Wallace is a little too hood for Shamar's taste.

They talk for a while before Shamar tells him he's got to get up early in the morning for work and ends the conversation.

For a few seconds Shamar thinks about jacking off and changes his mind. A little after one he slides in the king sized bed beside Cilana. She wakes up immediately. "You okay?" She asks.

"Yep. Come here." He kisses the side of her face. "I love you," Shamar says genuinely.

The bills are always going to be there. Cilana is always going to try too hard. They are going to get on each other's nerves--a lot. Marriage is sometimes a wonderful torture. Things might have been different had he waited until he was thirty to get married. But this is the life he's got. And it's not a bad life, either.

Cilana smiles and goes down on him for all of six minutes.

It's that nice mixed with the mean that keeps Cilana happy and stressed out with Shamar all the time.

Lost & Found

Bright sunlight shoots thru the shade-less and curtain-less window against Rain's face forcing her awake. She rises from the pillow she found thankfully last night in the dumpster and gets up from the trash ridden floor. Two mice sweep past her feet. She's named one Nicky and the other one, Micky.

"Daddy? Daddy!" She walks over to her father who is bent over in nothing but a dingy red tee shirt completely unconscious with the needle lying against the crease of his elbow. A few seconds later Rain has carefully removed the needle away from him with newspaper covering her fingers from the dried up blood. "Okay, dad, I'll be back from school around four, k?" she reminds him as though, somewhere in his wavering unconsciousness, he will hear her and remember.

Rain dashes down the stairs in her tattered, threadbare nightgown past Carlita Adams. Carlita is yelling and screaming once again. Carlita's apartment on the fifth floor—right below where Rain has lived the past three years, is the only other apartment other than hers that is not vacant in the abandoned building. There was a time she would go to Carlita's to change and get dressed since

Carlita's apartment somehow still has running water but after Kareem, Carlita's on again off again boyfriend, told Carlita he wanted to fuck Rain, Carlita told her she had to stop coming by. Carlita's only seventeen and Rain has known her for eight years—since Rain was four years old. That new dude, Kareem? Maybe Carlita's been with him for a year. But women like Carlita are always going to put a nigga before everything--before their children, before their mama, their job, their girlfriends—even though that same niggas would never go out of his way for them. Guys like him put their money first, their weed first, their mama, their boys—everything *except a woman* first. This Rain knows.

Running down the rest of the stairs, not stopping until she's at Paul's house, Rain takes in everything swimming past her. She loves to run and so far, for the last three years, she's been the fastest one on her middle school's track team. "Hey Pau-Pau." Paul is slow and can't say Pau*l*—only the Pau part.

"Heyyyy, Rai. Com-ing (come in)." Paul smiles, his arm clutched against his chest like a broken wing. Paul is maybe twenty? Rain still doesn't know. But he's been nice to her ever since she had to stop going to Carlita's and treats her as though she's his big sister. If he wasn't so tall you'd think he was around seven.

She showers, brushes her teeth and fixes her hair with a little gel into a puffy ponytail. The clothes she washed yesterday are dry and clean enough to wear to school today. Paul's got a mother somewhere but she's never home and doesn't mind Rain coming along as long as Rain doesn't start asking for too much or snooping around in her business and doesn't complain about not being able to come in on the mornings she is there with whatever guy has stayed the night.

Rain almost likes to think her mother looked something like Pau-Pau's mother. Denise has the remnants of a face that was once beautiful before the crack took its toll and Denise is sometimes nice. She always gets Rain a birthday gift from the dollar store, which is usually the only gift Rain gets all year. But Rain prefers to pretend her mother is some magnificent singer who is in some distant land and has lost her memory but will one day regain it and come back for her. That is better than knowing that she had to be removed prematurely from her mother who had OD-ed.

School is school. Rain tries not to ask too many questions when she doesn't catch something during English—math is her thing. Always a formula and always a right answer. That she can handle. But all that adjective and pronoun stuff drives her crazy. Most of the times, all goes well. No one notices the little brown girl with the growling stomach.

At lunch she sits by Consuela who will sometimes swap her homemade lunch for Rain's cafeteria stuff, school ends, there's track and then home—that is on the days she doesn't smell. Otherwise, on the days Denise tells her she can't come in, it's murder and she skips track. Coach Willis has already warned her twice about her "funk problem."

It's not the best kind of routine but it works. She knows what to count on all the rest of sixth grade. But come summer, everything changes. Their building catches fire, she can't find her dad for the next three days and somebody reports it and the final result, foster care, is worse than when the regular routine gets changed up.

First there is juvenile detention. Horrible, horrible juvie where girls like her either get forced to fuck the boys on the other floor or they have to sleep in bed with that big chick named Helena or get beaten up every day by whoever feels like fighting. Rain manages to escape it by sneaking back over to Denise's and Pau-Pau's until Denise starts thinking she'll get in trouble for it and stops letting Rain come in.

Carlita, still trying to hold on to Kareem, won't let her come over either even though she just got a nice place in these new low income apartments.

The only good thing—well, Rain hopes it's a good thing—is this family that has come to visit with her. They want her. The lady looks kind although it's kind of hard to tell. Rain always imagines mothers to be kind since she has never had one. The man, on the other hand makes Rain uneasy. She can't put her finger on it—there's something about him that makes her feel real uncomfortable.

They have a big house and live in a semi-nice neighborhood on the west side of Detroit. They have two kids of their own, a son they call RJ who's sixteen and another son they call Ralphie even though his name isn't Ralph. Then they've got three other adopted kids—a girl named Leslie who's thirteen, her ten-year old brother Tim and her little sister Timenia who's five.

The first couple of days start out okay. There's always breakfast, lunch and dinner, which Rain is very happy about. The mother, Mrs. Glenda, cooks pretty decent, they go to church, which is something Rain always wondered about and wanted to try. Church is fun, there's a lot of shouting and singing and they get to dress up a little for it. She has her own bunk bed—which is the first real bed she's ever slept on—outside of juvie. The only thing that slightly bothers her is how Mrs. Glenda makes them pour the Kool-Aid they don't finish back into the pitcher for later and how they have to eat the same thing the next meal if they don't like it and don't eat it the first time it's served; Rain has been served the same piece of liver for two days now and still can't manage to eat it. Over all, though, she likes it here.

But, after RJ starts coming into her room every night and won't stop and when Leslie starts tearing up Rain's new clothes, Rain starts hating that place. When she tells Mrs. Glenda, Mrs. Glenda only laughs it all off and tells her to stop being so sensitive. Mrs. Glenda also insist Rain and Leslie take baths together to save on water and even more terrible things happen there that Rain doesn't care to remember. Like RJ tying Rain up and making Ralphie lock her in the closet for hours when she fought back with RJ.

Finally, the social worker decides the situation isn't working out and puts Rain with this Black couple that live in Canton.

Their house looks real promising on the outside but inside is a different story. They are so filthy, so disgustingly dirty, Rain wants to cover her nose the entire time she's in the house—even the allies she used to get food out of dumpsters in didn't smell so bad. They have three huge dogs that terrorize Rain and bite her on a regular basis. The minute she comes home from school, after Rain finishes homework, the lady makes her clean until bedtime and when it's bedtime, the lady, who is bitterly angry her husband is always gone in the evening with his mistress but says nothing to her husband about it, she always has a lists of reasons Rain deserves to be spanked with belts and paddles.

The lady wakes Rain up in the morning by pounding her on her back. Rain hates her but still feels sorry for her. She knows the husband has three children with the mistress and that the lady cannot have children.

Rain finally leaves that house after a visit to the doctor and a look at her back and bottom.

After the fourth foster care home, at age fourteen, Rain runs away.

She steals enough money to catch the Greyhound to Ohio and leaves Detroit behind.

It feels good being in a totally new place. Being hungry and dirty with no place to go after the mall closes is the trade off. Rain has promised herself two things: to finish school and not to ever go back to foster care again. The first promise, finishing school, isn't as doable for the time being. With no address, no guardian--no nothing, she can't go to school. She will just be sent back to Michigan and back to juvie or another God-awful foster home.

Rain hasn't looked at herself in a mirror in a long time. She doesn't know that she is turning into a beautiful, beautiful young lady. She wouldn't know anyway, if she did look in a mirror. There has never been anyone to tell her.

After four days of sleeping on buses and in a shelter pretending to be eighteen, this girl with a slick honey-blonde weave named Starla approaches Rain in the shelter.

"Hey."

Rain briefly smiles back at her. One thing Rain has learned is that no one ever comes to you without an agenda. She is waiting to find out what Starla's is.

"You ain't eighteen—is you?" Starla strokes her slick honey-blonde weave.

"What?"

"You ain't godda play dumb wit me. You younger dan eighteen—I can tell…"

"I've godda go, sorry. I'll be back around at eight," Rains says.

"Stop playin' I ain't tryin' ta step at chu wrong. You younger. An' you musta been in a bad situation frum whereva you done came from cause I ain't neva seen no body eat so many bowls uh dat nasty ass cereal. …Look." Starla took Rain's hand. Rain wanted to jerk away but for some reason, didn't. "I'ma look out fa you. You up in here all by yo'self an' you showl act lost. But you smart--I can tell. I'ma help you. A girl like you don't need ta be up no place like dis."

Rain wants to ask Starla why she is in there if she can "help" but instead decides it would be best to act interested in whatever this chick is trying to game her on and then, find another place to stay tonight. It doesn't seem like Starla's gonna give up so quickly and Rain is getting a bad feeling.

"You see that nigga in dat gray Dodge Challenger ova dere?"

Rain nods yes.

"He wanna talk ta you. He cool. His name P Boy. He real cool peeps--he'll git you where you tryin' ta go."

"Well why are you at the shelter if you know him and he can help *me* get out of here?"

Starla just laughs and shakes her head at Rain's innocence. "You silly. Gon' on ova dere an' talk ta him. He like you. He like you a lot."

The tinted window rolls down and the dude, P Boy, gives her a smile. He clicks open his door and Rain hops in. She should be scared. But P Boy is as fine as he is dark and—in all honesty—doesn't turn her stomach. They stare at each other for a few seconds.

"Ma bad, ma bad—P Boy." He reaches out his hand for a handshake, which is weird to Rain but convinces her even more so that this dude is a cool cat. "I peeped you the otha day. You fine as hell, you know dat?" he asks smirking her way. "Where you from?"

Rain stares out the window.

"Okay, okay. So, I done caught chu off guard. I'll go first den. I'm uh money maker, I'm eighteen, I been doing ma thang foe uh while and—what else you wanna know?"

Rain still says nothing. She wants to get out of the car now but…there is nowhere else to go.

"You ain't no undacover po-po, is you?"

Rain half smiles and shakes her head no.

"Well, I'll give you time ta check me out. I know I'm coming on kinda strong and whatnot, but I like you…whatchu got up taday?"

Rain shrugs.

"Why 'on't you roll wit me foe uh few, I'll bring you back here."

Rain looks at him and nods yes.

P Boy takes her to a restaurant in the mall, a real sit down restaurant. Rain has never been to one. Then, he buys her a couple of outfits he says are "real fly foe uh bitch like her." They talk—well, he talks and tells her he's never met a chick as quiet as her. But, as promised, he brings her back to the shelter—no incident tried, which makes Rain suspicious. Is he using her as a cover up for something?

It's still the same routine three weeks later—only, she's been to P Boy's crib and watched movies with him and he still hasn't pushed up on her. He always just takes her back to the shelter at the end of the evening. This is the last day she has at the shelter without any problems. She's at the part she heard somebody call "transition" and soon, they'll be asking her questions and trying to help her find a place and a job. She doesn't know what'll happen if she tells them the truth. She wishes they'd just let her stay at the shelter.

"Look, why 'on't chu stay here from now on?" P Boy propositions.

Rain thinks about it for all of a half an hour before agreeing.

"I godda make uh run, though. You ma girl from now on so, sometimes when I make uh run, I want chu ta roll wit me."

Rain nods yes.

After his run, P Boy takes Rain for a drive. He shows her all the places he's lived and tells her more about himself. His mother was an addict like Rain's mother only he never knew his dad. He tells her about how he's been a runner since he was seven and how the mob hooked him up. "I ain't neva told no bitch all da shit I'm tellin' you, Rain. Respect dat."

And Rain will. Before this, she had never even thought about love or one day having children. But P Boy is so unexpected, so what she needs right now—and fine as hell. Everything about him, his style, the way he talks, the way he looks at her, she's feeling.

That night Rain comes on to him as they sit in his truck in a parking spot at the park. And it's better, it's so good, it takes away some of the pain she always linked with men and love since she was twelve.

...It gets to where P Boy completely trust Rain at his crib when he does runs and everybody in town knows she's P Boy's Princess. The other chicks that used to call the house don't call anymore and not because she had to go off on P—all because *he* decided he only needed to be with *her*. And Rain is so good at math, she's good on the books. Sometimes, because she likes it so much, they go to church. They've gone out of town—once to Denver on one of P's runs and another time to Cali. It's nice not having to worry about meals or clothes or running water. But what's even nicer is the way P always calls and tells Rain he loves her and the way he's always gentle when they make love.

The only real issue they've had is the miscarriage thing. This is the second time Rain's gotten pregnant and P Boy really wants her to have his child. He's starting to think Rain could be having abortions but she's always at home or either with him. They try and try but still Rain isn't pregnant. Rain wants his baby but she's still worried about school. She's been out a whole year. She could go right now and still be okay, she thinks. She started preschool when she was three—her dad wanted to put her somewhere while he was off getting high.

She's unsure, though. What if she gets hooked on P's supply? What if one day she tries it, and then likes it so much she ODs and her baby has to be cut out, too? What if she ends up being just like her dad? It can't be that simple and easy—being a parent, she'd seen so many bad ones in and out of foster care—she'd rather not have children if it meant turning into such a wicked entity. Entity… The first time she used that word everyone in class thought she was trying to say titty. Sixth graders were stupid. People were stupid. Parents were stupid.

Everything is going better than well with P Boy; she really does want to give him a baby. All his homeboys have at least two—by different girls. All P wants is one baby by her.

They keep trying and having fun trying but still no baby.

They begin to travel more and one day P comes home and tells Rain they're buying a new house. "It's time, baby. And I wont chu ta help me pick it, too. The business and God been good ta me. We gon' git us a house and maybe in the next year I'll be able to chop up da game and put ma money inta uh barber shop." That's all P talks about, one day owning a barbershop.

They get a nice little house in Cleveland, two hundred thousand g's—not too flashy—just like P wanted and everything is going really, really well. P's only a few months away from being able to chill and go to barber college. Rain's never seen him so happy. He's always in what he calls a "chipper" mood these days. He's already been hanging out at the Shop a couple of blocks down and learning the basics.

"I'ma be hot ta death in school! I already know how ta fade and do—" P is interrupted by a loud banging sound, then something that could only be gunfire. P looks at Rain and without a word, P signals for her to leave or hide just like they'd practiced and discussed in case of a situation like this.

But Rain doesn't want to leave P's side. She'd rather be dead than without him. But P doesn't want her to see him in a situation like this and he signals again for her to leave. Rain's always done what P's told her to do because P's never done anything other than look out for her. At this point, with four of the niggas that have been trying to shut P's business down for the last three years all the way in the kitchen, there isn't time for Rain—who is now on the back porch--to leave. They will hear the door open. She walks lightly all the way to the basement and hides in the crawl space that looks like part of the wall to one unknowing.

She can faintly hear them beating P. She hears moans. Loud, horror filled moans. Lots of banging. Questions—they ask him questions that he refuses to answer. This goes on for the rest of the day. At night when she can't hear anything anymore Rain is still too afraid to move. Is P still upstairs? Is he still alive? She uses the tiny flashlight in the emergency kit to check her watch and waits half a day before un-balling herself from the crawlspace only to find P in a pool of blood with a knife still stuck slightly in his back. His head is so swollen it looks like a red and brown pillow instead of his face. She holds him against her chest screaming and screaming. She kisses P's swollen body still screaming. Just as she begins to really go crazy, it happens. P moans a slow and hard groan.

"B*aaab*y!" Rain runs to the phone but it is dead. She goes to the neighbor's house and uses the phone to call 911 and a few minutes later P is on the way to the nearby emergency room.

Rain stays the night in the waiting room. They won't let her come in. For the next month P remains in the hospital. They had done so many terrible things to him, his lung had been partially punctured, two of his ribs have been broken… It was a miracle he was still alive; she had prayed he was still alive.

Finally when they allow him visitors, Rain goes everyday to sit with P until visiting hours end. Sometimes she even slides in the bed with him and holds his hand and prays and sings him his favorite gospel songs. He taps his fingers against her hand sometimes. Other times he looks at her and faintly smiles. He was right about her—that time he saw her carrying that small backpack. Even in those raggedy clothes he could tell. That was why they'd wanted him to get her to hook for ole boy Motley since P had owed him a couple hundred g's. P Boy was always the one to talk anybody into anything. They knew he'd get her and, with that face and body, she'd be a moneymaker. But P had insisted against it and paid them back by working a little harder and getting a few new young dudes to join his crew.

Rain was gonna be his. He knew he loved Rain the moment she had sat in his car.

Everything would have been back to normal—whatever normal was after a situation like that. But instead of going home once he's released, the police are waiting outside P's room. Rain is there kicking and screaming something terrible.

Court dates and more court dates before the final verdict. Twenty-five to life. Rain didn't know all the things P had done until now. The dog fights, the little kids working for him, the prostitution ring—he never discussed any of it with her. But none of that could ever change her love for him. Rain would lie down and die if P told her to.

A lot of what is happening Rain can't understand—all the loquacious law vernacular and lingo—she can't understand any of it. There is something about bail. Two hundred thousand? Was that what the judge had said? That was what that man, the one in the navy suit, that semi-bald, obese Italian one, had said when she finally stepped out of the courtroom.

What Rain didn't know was that they were still vying for her to pay P's debt. No matter how much he paid them, they found more ways to up it so he still owed them and ended up owing them even more. Too bad P hadn't had Rain checking those other books for him—she would have caught that. Although P told Rain almost everything, he didn't want her worried about all the 'extra' business. Rain was real sweet and real Godly and she would have been pushing him to get out. P was already stressed. He didn't need his girl starting in on him, too.

Really, right now there is no way Rain can pay P's way out of federal prison. And even though this lawyer dude is looking real slick to her right about now, she won't go to another lawyer to ask questions. Rain isn't going to do anything she isn't sure P would want her to do.

She's seen this guy a few times in pictures P's had stored away in his safe. She's still unsure, very unsure, but accepts the invitation to dinner with this Motley dude. Everything about him annoys her. His greasy hair, the fact that she knows his real name isn't Motley, the way he laughs while gazing at her chest. But P would want her to go with him, wouldn't he? And she wants her man out of the federal penitentiary. Already she's losing the house; it was in P's name. P had no proof of earned income and there is more legal shit she doesn't understand. Already she was getting threatening phones calls in the middle of the night, some "tell where the rest of it is or else" crap.

P had never warned her about any mess like this.

"You know, you coulda been in big trouble, too, Rain..."

She's not going to ask what Motley means. This fat mouthed, grease ball is going to give her all the info she needs. She can tell.

"We got ya' finga prints on some things... We've seen you handling the business, if you know what I mean," he leans in and says right before giving a vile grin and laugh.

The rest of the dinner grows more and more uncomfortable. But nothing happens after that except Rain goes home scared to death because someone has been in the house. She can't tell whether or not the person is still there.

At the last minute she decides to go to Roxanne's house—a girl from church she's become kind of cool with, which is the best thing she could have done. The next day, when she goes by her house to check it, it is burned to the ground. All the memories, all the furniture P had spent a good grip on, all their clothes, the baby stuff they'd bought, the pictures—all of it burned to crisp ashes on the ground.

"Girl, you can stay wit me," Roxanne, who rode with her, offers. "I could use tha help if you gon' put sumthen on my rent."

"Girl, I really appreciate it," Rain replies still not wanting to believe any of this is real, P going to prison, the house… The last thing on her mind is how she was going to pay rent or buy food or how she is simply going to make it day to day.

Rain's phone rings. "Hey, Rain." It's Motley again. This sucker just won't stop. All day, every hour calling and calling telling her more shit that she doesn't understand supposedly about P's case.

"You see what we can do?" Motley laughs again. "I'ma tellin' you, honey. You need to work with me, not against me. You work with me? You *beautiful-uh-liffe*! You work againsta me, not so *beautiful-uh-liife*!"

Rain doesn't say anything.

"Meet me, twelve o' five, near the docks. Lose the chick ya' got witcha." And that's it, Motley hangs up. only Rain is sure that was not Motley. It is definitely someone else, someone older, like seventy-ish and who has smoked more than his fair share of cigars in his lifetime."

I've been thru worse, I can handle this. As long as P's alive, I've got to do whatever I can to get him out. Everything is gonna turn out okay, Rain silently repeats. Her hands are so shaky she has to pull over and let Roxanne, whose license is suspended and who she took with her against the caller's directive, drive back to Roxanne's house.

"I'll--I'll be right back Roxi. I godda make a run," Rain tells her as she drops Roxanne off. When Roxi goes in the house, Rain pulls over at the next stop sign and prays for a good while. The same stuff: *God help P, let me get him out, make all this stop, just let us be able to move on with our lives, let him get his shop and let us just have normal, regular lives, God. I'm not asking for all the money in the world, I'm not asking for nothing except for P to be okay, God. Let me have his child, let everything work out good. Please! In Jesus name, Amen, Lord! Please!*

Rain is there at the docks. She can't remember the ride there. She is in a daze. Her spirit is telling her this man is not right. But she is calm now. She's not thinking about anything other than getting P out--soon.

"Yah, yah, good ta see you. You always did follow directions well, Rain." Motley runs his hand against her behind. Rain tenses. "Here's all you godda do. Tamarro, show up at Larry's Place. Dress nice—wear sumen nice. You hang around wit us big dogs for uh lil while, ya live uh good life. You'll hava fun. Just for uh little while and I make good on P. I make it easy. You be good? He be good. You 'stand what I'ma sayin'? See you at ten." And that was all. Motley wobbles himself into a pizza delivery van and drives off.

Rain cannot sleep. She stays up the whole night thinking about what the judge had said, what the lawyers said and going back and forth on this whole Motley thing. He never said for how long or what she'd be doing... And what if he didn't honor his word? But. If this *was* the only way to get P out, she would have to do it. She had to.

P would do anything for her if the situation was flipped.

When Rain arrives at Larry's Place this tall, attractive blonde haired, white girl in a navy dress with a gleaming diamond necklace dazzling around her thin neck opens the bar and quickly ushers her upstairs. The hallway is gloomy and a vomit green color. The blonde girl knocks twice, pauses then knocks two more times.

A cheap looking white girl accompanied by a cheap looking black chick rush to greet Rain after the door flings open. "Hi, honey. Sit down, Big Larry been waiting foe you." Starla. The way she moves and writhes about, she looks like a shoddy, cracked-out, floozy siren. There are fifty dollar ones and there are four thousand dollar an hour Russian and Thailand ones—the special ones. Somehow Rain figures she is caught in between.

For the next three months Rain will do many, many things she's never imagined. Things that turn her stomach. She will say P's name before and after and do it, mindlessly while shedding silent tears in the process.

The last time she ever does anything like this again it is Stevie. On this day she is so unaffected, feeling so nonexistent, nothing matters anymore. Except P. The guy comes to the Hilton room at the exact given time. She stands up and opens the door. "OOOh, you got a nice one–good thing, too. I asked for a nice one." Rain doesn't know what's going on. She hadn't gotten a call for two. "Yeah, this is my son. His mother's gotten all weird and all into this new religion—Jehovah's Witness crap. Man, those are a buncha weirdo's if I've ever seen any. Well, since she's taking him he's been turning more and more into a weirdo. He's never really been a ladies man like his ole man." The suburban fifty something white guy laughs into Rain's face, "So I want my boy to have a good time today—show him a few things, help him out a little bit. You know? ...Ooh, you're nice. If I had the time, I'd say you and *me*. But—well, I godda get back home to the wife, ya' know. I'll be downstairs in two hours. That good son?"

The son lowers his red face in severe shame and shuts the door on his father. Rain and Stevie sit on the edge of the bed. Stevie traces the quilted pattern on the comforter for a while before speaking. "I'm embarrassed of him."

Rain gives a quick nod. "I guess we all are embarrassed of our parents."

"...I don't wanna do anything."

"That's cool. Turn on the TV..."

But Stevie would rather talk. "I guess I *am* weird. A total dork—you could say. I don't watch TV that much. Nobody likes me at school. I love going to the hall. I read the bible a lot..."

"That's cool. Nobody likes me much either. I used to read the bible all the time. But I *do* like to watch TV." Rain laughs so tempted to turn on the television anyway. She hasn't watched it in almost a month.

"I bet people hate me more than they hate you!" Stevie teases.

"Impossible. I've only met two people that liked me. Your parents like you and I'm sure there are a few other people so...I win." With that they both slightly laugh.

"I can't imagine anyone not liking you," Stevie adds. "Besides, I hate my dad. He's a cop. He cheats on my ma and he's always trying to get me to be a *man's man*-- life sucks."

"...Tell me about it." Rain tells him the short of the long about her life. Until now the only person that's ever known anything of any real substance about her is P. She kind of feels guilty for sharing this with Stevie the minute she finishes. He will probably really think she is black trash now.

"...That's not cool..." He says shaking his head. Five minutes after their time is up his dad knocks on the door. "Wait a sec—don't go anywhere, okay?" Stevie asks Rain.

As his dad yell obscenities in the hallway Rain turns the television up. After forty minutes or so the phone rings. It's Motley. "Yeah, you're gonna be going wit the dude and Stevie. Great workin' with ya. You musta really done sumthen nice! You musta really shown 'em a good time, no? Take care Lil Darlin'!"

Rain is slightly confused until Stevie comes back in.

"I've got dirt on my dad. I told him you're coming

with us. I mean…like you could go back to school or something…and my mom rents places out so…"

Rain can't hear anything else he is saying. Within seconds she is hugging him then she rushes to the bathroom and washes the crap off her face Motley made her wear and changes into a t-shirt and jeans. It is too good to be true but nothing could be worse than her current situation.

The entire ride to the suburbs, Stevie's dad, Rich, is surly. His cheeks are beet red.

Stevie is explaining things to his mother and leaving out a lot of details. He puts her on the phone with Rain.

"Hi, honey! Rain, is it?"

"Yes."

"My son tells me you're awesome but in a bit of trouble and that you're really interested in the bible?"

"Yes, I am."

"Well, I'd love to meet you. Hopefully we can talk and figure something out."

"K."

When she hangs up he whispers to Rain, "I'm blackmailing my dad. I've got tons of dirt on 'im. You're good. Watch." For this Rain will forever appreciate Stevie.

An hour later she is meeting Mrs. Catherine Lowalski. Catherine, as she prefers Rain to call her, is a cute, dainty curly haired blonde who is super cheery. Rain wants to think she is a bit dingy but has decided against it since she is genuinely nice and believes Rain is twenty-one instead of sixteen. She even rents her one of her studio apartments on Court Drive which is in walking distance to the mall and Catherine helps Rain get a job working with her at The Naturalizer at the mall. Rain kept her fake license and social security card Motley had given her. Actually, it was a real license. Some girl named Brandi who looked very similar to Rain. They claimed she had left but everyone knew the girl was "missing" because she tried escaping. They all had tethers but somehow Brandi had slipped hers off and was almost out of the window when they busted in on her after a client. Word had it Brandi's face was so messed up she might as well been dead. Completely seared. Features fused together…

Rain is studying the bible with Catherine and will soon be baptized into the Jehovah's Witnesses faith. She wonders what P would say about this. It is definitely different from the church she and he used to go to on Sundays. Still, life is finally normal with one exception. She would really like to finish high school and with all the talk Steve does about college when he visits her apartment on the weekends, she's thinking she wants to major in accounting—get a Masters degree even. She's already looked up night school options.

There is a small regret that she will not be able to go to regular high school—she is only sixteen. She's never had the chance to do anything normal—not even the chance to grow up in a normal way. That has begun to bother her more and more. *But things like that shouldn't bother me*, she reminds herself. This is her one shot at being normal—eventually.

After saving up and getting an old school Mark VII, Rain goes to see P one Friday afternoon. She's gotten the directions, given Catherine and Steve a top-notch excuse and arrives on schedule. She's written him seven letters and they agreed she would come see him today.

But something is wrong. Gravely wrong. P never comes out. Rain asks the guard if there is some mistake but there are too many people there, too much going on and no one cares whether an inmate gets a visit or not. She has driven all the way to Virginia in that unreliable car of hers. It stopped two times on the way. She is so hurt, it is like someone just sliced half of her heart away. Had he heard she slept with all those guys? Had he? What if he didn't want her now? P had always said he would never see her the same if she ever cheated on him… Didn't he know she did it for him? What happen to "Pain and Rain til the end of time?" That was what he had always said, that he would always love her no matter what.

Rain doesn't want to go back to Ohio but she has to. What other options are there? Besides, Catherine has been a sweetie pie and Steve—such a nerdy white boy—is her one true friend. He's much more of a friend than Roxanne had ever been. Roxanne made her pay an exorbitant twelve hundred a month for rent, car usage, food, electricity and water usage even though her rent was only six hundred a month. That had eaten up all the money Rain had been able to salvage from the stash P had given her. Steve and Catherine had never been like that. Rich was still brusque and always threatening Rain not to say anything to Catherine who wouldn't have believed anything ill of him anyway. But that didn't matter. Rain hardly ever dealt with Rich. In an area where most white folks thought any sign of brown was property tarnishment for sure, Catherine had proudly carried her to the kingdom hall and practically anywhere else Rain felt like accompanying Catherine. It was time to give up on P. He would never see her the same anyway. P had given up on her.

But when Rain gets back to Ohio there is one major glitch. Rich has looked up info on Rain and found out her real age. He's told Catherine a total butt covering story in the hopes of getting her out of his hair—just in case she is trouble in the long run. Some things have been coming out in the precinct. He needs to keep his gate closed. The less they can dig up on him, the better.

Surprisingly to Rich, Rain comes clean. She tells Catherine about her childhood and the whole foster care bit. Of course she leaves out the P part and that whole Motley thing and how she actually met Steve and Rich. And, of course, Rich appreciates that because he still isn't sure Catherine isn't on to him. It's like that when you lead a double life. The guilt one usually feels corrodes the mind to the actual happenings of things.

Catherine cries profusely. But not for the reasons Rain thinks. Rain thinks she will be arrested for fraud or something of the like. She thinks she will be on the evening news or in jail or that Rich will send her back to Motley. Instead, Catherine takes Rain's face in her hands and says, "You, poor, poor thing. I admire your courageousness. I am *so sorry* any of those things happened to you."

Steve had already gone back to his room and has his headphones on and is on SoundCloud. He hates to hear Rain tell the story. It makes him sick although he would never admit it.

Within weeks Catherine has arranged to be Rain's legal guardian and finishing school is top priority next to bible study. Rain moves in with them and finds it anomalous Rich doesn't seem to mind.

The next good thing is Rain gets to go to normal high school. She would be three good years behind but after testing she is only being held back a year. When given the option of being held back a year versus going to night school, Rain immediately jumps at regular high school.

It is exactly what she expects. Nice. This time her stomach doesn't growl. She doesn't have to worry about being "Dat Stanky Girl" or "The Pee Pee B." She doesn't mind being one of the only blacks in school. This state of normalcy is priceless.

She still has a hard time with English—all the reading and whatnot but Steve is a pretty darn good tutor. She teaches him how to be a little more "cool" in exchange for the homework help. People really like her. She even winds up with a boyfriend—this boy who tries to act black named Bryce. Bryce, although not as cool as P, is totally every girl's crush in the ninth, tenth and eleventh grades. Rain is back into running track and now going out of state for competitions. The only thing about that is Catherine thinks Rain should be devoting more time out in field service knocking on doors to do preaching work instead of being on the track team. And Rain cannot do anything outside of school with Bryce because he is not a Jehovah's Witness.

Steve has held up his promise as far as not telling Catherine about Bryce but he really can't stand Bryce. Bryce used to clown him in the hallways and still picks on him. He doesn't see how Rain can stand the guy.

Steve and a lot of chicks hoped they broke up after all the chasing each other in hallways and wearing matching colors. This somehow lasts until graduation.

Somewhere during Steve's senior year and Rain's junior year of undergrad, the sidelong glances became more noticeable. Rain had already turned down three young brothers at the kingdom hall down. Jehovah's Witnesses even in their area usually didn't go away to college but Rich was totally against the idea of them commuting to college at home. He pressured Rain and Steve to go away which ended up being in state but still away enough to keep Steve from being one of those boys who never moved out. Something had to toughen the boy up, in Rich's opinion.

Understandably, Rich was terribly surprised when he came up to the campus on an emergency regarding Catherine. Steve didn't look as scrawny, his voice had quit sounding like Screech's from *Saved by the Bell* and he had even taken Rich up on a game of hoops. It was weird. Like he had finally almost gotten the son he had been deprived of.

At first Rich thought they were more like brother and sister—the joshing, jokes at each other's expense, the way they seemed to need breaks from each other. But then, after taking another look at the way Steve would gently touch Rain's hand or watch her walk off when he thought no one else was looking—it all started to make sense.

Rich knew before Steve or Rain realized it. Catherine had already recognized it the day Steve brought her home like an exotic cat he'd rescued from the lost-&-

found waiting to be relinquished from a life of less finery than what she was accustomed.

Catherine knew there would one day be this exact a time when Steve told her he had something to tell her but neither knew how the other would take it. Catherine thought it might be worse. Him being away with all those worldly folks—that Steve and Rain might find themselves in an illicitly immoral quandary of some sort. Steve had started erasing the history on his phone due to all the links to Pornhub on it from the time he was thirteen…

Instead they went to the justice of the peace one day and then called a week later and admitted they skipped summer classes and were instead on their honeymoon in Denver. Rain had picked Denver because of that one time P took her. Not that she missed P as tragically anymore. It was just that Denver had been so beautiful. It had been her first real trip. This time with Steve, it was just as wonderful as she remembered. They went camping and he took her to a few ice skating shows. She always secretly wished she could have been an ice skater. Once she told Steve that when he was sixteen. Somehow he had remembered. That was one of those special things about him.

They thought it would be too strange to get married at the kingdom hall. Not that they hadn't kept things morally chaste. No, they had never done anything outside of kissing before the I Do's. Well, one time Steve had peeked in the shower on her. And she'd caught him jacking off back in the day when she first moved in. Nice size for a skinny white boy back then. Even better now that he had grown into himself!

The oddest thing happens, however. Steve gets a job offer based in Detroit. He would be over a new hotel development there. Rain is not too happy about this whole business of going back to that city. She feels like her past is a book now closed. But the job offers magnificent perks and benefits. Timeshares paid for on the Virgin Islands and in LA, free airfare allowances, excellent health benefits... The plan is for him to start his job while she is in her last year of college. "You can always take grad classes in Michigan, if you'd like," Steve constantly reminds her. He always has a look of enthusiasm whenever the whole job out of state thing comes up.

"But we haven't even been married a year! I don't like this long distance thing!" Rain always argues.

"How long have we known each other? Do you trust me?" Steve asks for probably the sixtieth time.

"Yeah...whatever. Okay. Take the job! Goodness gracious!" She finally gives in. But they both make concessions. She finishes her last year of school in Michigan and starts grad school at Wayne State University (which she has ambivalent feelings about. It wasn't a nice sentiment—being reminded on a weekly basis of how your dad used to be slumped over next to the old Marwill's bookstore begging for spare change across from what was now Barnes and Noble and the Welcome Center).

At first it was Catherine incessantly in Steve's ear, "Absence makes the heart grow fonder of somebody else! Besides, I love Rain and I want grandkids. You can't leave her here in Ohio, Stevie!"

Then Rain gets offered a job working for Bank of America as a junior accounting administrative executive.

Actually that was what sealed their move to Michigan. Steve would be traveling constantly anyway so if Rain had stayed in Ohio or moved it really wouldn't have mattered. He planned on coming to see her once every two weeks regardless.

So they move into a brownstone off Woodward not too far from the Fox Theater. With a decked-out home, a job Rain really, really loves (she stays as late as possible on the nights Steve is out of town), they go out of town together once every month and Steve has just become a ministerial servant at the kingdom hall which couldn't make Catherine any happier. Life is good for everyone involved—even Rich who has finally retired from cheating on his wife and the force. He's studying to become a Jehovah's Witness and it's Catherine's dream come true. So what if he is only doing it because he's entitled to being the "head of the house and, therefore, rule maker." That is the one true thing he likes about their whole religious ideology.

Things should stop here. They really should. But then the other part of the story would go untold.

It wasn't exactly a good year after all roads moved them to Michigan. A strange letter came rolled up in an odd brown package—one of those packages architects use to protect their blueprints. The moment Rain saw it lying against the storm door her chest twitched and a muscle spasm shook something awful in her right calf leg. For a whole day she just ignored them—the continuous muscle spasm and the package.

Steve wasn't home. She could wait until he came home tomorrow to open it. But that was stupid and she was twenty-three for heaven's sake. Why was she acting so scared about nothing?

After opening it, she threw it on hallway floor and went into the kitchen. Wine. She needed some wine. An hour later she unrolled it.

A large, beautiful drawing of her face—the way she used to look. The way she only half smiled. Then there was another sheet behind it of three different poems. Then a letter.

Why didn't people know when to leave good enough alone? Why did P pick *this* particular time to try to reconnect? Niggas, niggas, niggas. That was almost ten years ago. Didn't people in prison know in real time that things changed within ten *long* years?

She wanted to and she meant to throw it out but she didn't. And she didn't mention it to Steve either. Instead, she felt so guilty for keeping anything from Steve she tried to make things extra special that night. From how hard Steve slept afterwards she must have succeeded in showing him just how much she loved him and missed him.

But P just wouldn't stop. And her avoidance, the fact that she ignored every last package he sent only edged him on. They became so frequent she began throwing them out—all except the first two.

"Ay yo! Guess, who? Why you been avoiding me, ma?" A year and a half later she got the call. Ronya had interrupted her right in the middle of an important presentation and report with the senior executives. Two of the execs had flown in.

"Important!" Ronya insisted. "He won't stop calling. He says he must speak with you."

Rain's blood pressure shot up with the thought of something happening to Steve.

But it was P. "Look, ma. I found you on LinkedIn and Thatsthem.com. I'm in Michigan. I need to talk to you. I'm out and I'm here. Meet me in Greektown when you finish whatever that lady just said you were doing."

"I—I can't leave!" She had no reason to say anything. She could have just hung up but she was caught off guard and unable to think temporarily.

Rain did lunch with the senior director of quality control Marsha Maze who was an amazing thirty-something sista who wore long, neat Sisterlocks and saw so much potential in Rain from day one at the Tennessee Leadership Forum she'd recruited Rain for Bank of America.

Steve called and gave a detailed run down of the "most annoying day of his life" (which was nice because usually he was a man of few words. This was the first time he talked for thirty minutes in one phone conversation).

Her best friend Lindsey had called and invited her to a concert tonight. Things were so normal.

Sometimes just plain ole normal is perfect.

On the way out of her office at the Renaissance she smiled reviewing her day. On the way to the Riverwalk as she always did when the weather was nice she bought buttered popcorn and a Dasani water from the guy who had a stand. And there sat P on the cement bench where she usually sat.

The popcorn spilled all over the ground. The water fell out of her now opened hand and her mouth hung open as wide as her eyes now were.

"Come sit down next ta me, girl. I just wanna look at you. Ms. Corporate now, hungh? You doin' it Big Willie style, now!"

"I came to see you in the prison and you—you didn't even come out!" she blurted in sheer anger.

"I sent a letter to you at Roxy's. They changed the date. They didn't let me come out!"

"You know what? STAY THA FUCK AWAY FROM ME—P!" she shouted and ran all the way to the inside of the Renaissance. After grabbing her purse out of her office, she got her car from valet and drove home.

The more she thought about it the more pissed off she became. She went to the store and bought a whole pack of Djarum cigars and almost lost her religion on them. She never smoked before this and it didn't feel or taste good. That was exactly what seeing P after all these years was like. It didn't feel good.

That night she stayed in her navy pants suit and blouse. Didn't wipe off the eyeliner, which was now a smudgy mess. Didn't turn on the television. Instead she drunk damn near a gallon of Hennessey on the rocks—which was hardcore for her. She'd always mixed it with Pepsi.

For the first time ever she called off work. She never missed a day of school from the time Catherine had found out her real age. She had never missed a day of her undergrad or grad courses or work. Work was the thing she loved so much only second to Steve. She never had any real female friends until she got this job.

She lay on the couch the entire night and smudged it with tears and Stila liquid eyeliner and mascara and Hennessey sobs.

"GO THA FUCK AWAY!"

"Oh, you cussin' like a lil white girl now, hungh?" P showed up at her door like he was the UPS man on regular package delivering business. "I'll always find you."

"I wrote you letters, you never responded. Life is good now. I'm married and I'm happy. If you love me just *go away*," she whispered thru the steady stream of tears.

"I didn't get your letters. They took everything away from me. The niggas that got me had pull like that, ma. Didn't you— " she slammed the door in his face before he had the chance to say anything else.

In five hours Steve would be back from San Diego. All of this P stuff was irrelevant at this point.

But just because one person gives up on love doesn't mean the other party will or should.

Steve hadn't been in the house an hour when Rain heard a noise. It sounded like something was scratching against the door. Steve beat her to the door—Rain was in the kitchen fixing salad and heating up the crabcakes and Cajun rice Steve had brought home.

"That was strange," Steve muttered closing the door with Rain right behind him. And for the rest of the evening her mind wheeled in circles with the thought of P coming on purpose when Steve was home.

For two consecutive weeks P showed up at the Riverwalk at the bench and didn't run into her. After that he started showing up next to the valet where she left her Audi. "What I godda do to show you how I feel 'bout chu, Rain?" The feelings were intense in his eyes.

"P? What do you want from me? What'll make you stop showing up and trying to ruin my life?"

"Damn, baby. Ta hear you say some shit like that, like I'm ruining yo' life kinda takes tha wind out uh nigga, you know what I'm sayin'? I still love you, though. Ain't gone never stop… 'Member dat time I took you shoppin' right after we met? 'Member dat?"

"…Yes…"

"I used ta 'member how yo' eyes would light up when you was happy whenever I was having it rough when I was locked up…"

Rain shouldn't but she lets herself remember that day. She remembers how fine P looked and thinks about how he is still just as nice looking—even after that terrible beating. "Well I have to go and you can't stand next to my car forever. I really loved you. I loved you *hard*. Now when I look back I was put in a terrible situation for a whole year because—"

"--SSSssh. I know, I know. That's one of the reasons I have to make it right. They already told me what went down when I was gone. I'm willing to do whatever I need to do about that. I have some plans about that and—"

"--P? Don't go trying to kill somebody over that. It's over." She could still read his mind.

They stood there for a good twenty minutes before he took it upon himself to open her car door and sit in the passenger's seat. Without thinking about it, Rain opened the driver's side and sat down. "I wont you ta have my baby. That's all I wont. I'll step back. Do you. But I wont you ta have my child. That's what I always wonted. Foe real…" And he opened the door, got out of the truck and walked away without looking back.

Steve was gone too much. Rain never seemed to notice until now. He didn't always return her calls…she never wondered if he had ever cheated on her until now. Catherine would call every night around ten. Kind of felt like Catherine might be checking in on her. When he came home everything was fine…but lately Steve had been tired more than two days in a row when Rain had rolled over and tried to get something started.

Then there was that receipt she found—dinner for *two*. Three rounds of wine. Hmm… There was some chick he kept mentioning—Ping, an Asian chick. She was a good bet for that damn dinner date. Dinner, which totaled *a hundred and sixty dollars*.

"Baby? Are you cheating on me?" Rain couldn't stop herself from asking on the way to the kingdom hall Sunday morning.

"WHAT? Are you serious?"

"You didn't answer the *fuckin'* question?"

He pulled over and stared at her a couple for a minute. "You can quit your job and come with me when I travel and—"

"--STOP IT WITH THE SARCASM, ALREADY! YOU'RE CHEATING ON ME, AREN'T YOU? JUST

SAY IT! I'M NOT GONNA QUIT MY JOB! I COULD'VE JUST STAYED IN OHIO IF IT WAS GONNA BE LIKE THIS!"

"I'm reading the Watchtower today. I can cancel so we can go home and talk if you'd like—"

"--Quit trying to be so nice about it! Are you cheating? It's a yes or no question. That's all I wanna know, dammit!"

Some women make the mistake of thinking men don't have emotions. It's all right there in a man's eyes. You can tell when he loves a woman by the tone of his voice in times like these as well.

Steve had always thought Rain too well adjusted for all the crap life had imposed upon her. He had even talked her into getting counseling at college but she acted the same. Quiet for the most part. A little laid back. Funny lots of times, though. Furtively he always expected her to snap about something at some point. They only had diminutively small arguments the entire time they knew each other—*you said you saved it on the Hulu! Why did you forget?*--stuff like that. Usually Rain refused to argue. He was surprised to know she was suspicious.

Instead of going to the hall, they went home and made up in a way that almost convinced Rain.

But, not quite.

She was thinking during the second round about how Ping had called two days in a row. It pissed her off so much she faked the next orgasm. Quite frankly *faking* was something she had never found necessary with her husband until tonight.

The smoke was still there but nothing was roasting. It had been seven months with no incident and no corporeal signs of P.

Steve calmed down his travels but not necessarily because of Rain's accusation. There was a major project in accordance with the whole "revival of the city" project.

He had planned on trying to be more stationary in the upcoming years, though. He and Rain had discussed when they wanted to start a larger family on their honeymoon. Rain had said around twenty-five was good for her. That gave him a good year to work things out as far as switching job positions was concerned.

His dad had been one of the most racist men he had ever met yet he'd still slept with black chicks.

Steve never thought about any of that until now.

His child would be mixed. It was weird. People always said you didn't see a person's color but that wasn't true. You did. Steve had never thought of Rain as white. And he never thought of her as black either. Still, even though he liked her from the very start—she was the only one that had caught his eye out of all the pictures he flipped thru that God-awful day his father took him to that place.

He never really thought of Rain in terms of her color. He only ever thought of her in terms of his dream girl.

"Hey, babe. What are you up to? You feel like taking off the rest of the day and meeting me at home?" Steve left a message since her phone was off.

When Rain got home Steve had set the mood with flowers, candles, her favorite carryout and he was in the Jacuzzi waiting. That night everything felt so right, even though she had skipped the birth control pills a whole week by mistake she couldn't resist staying on top and watching his face.

"God, I love you," she whispered into his ear.

Had things not gone so well that one day, had there been an excuse like a bad, bad argument turned violent or something, it could possibly not be so bad.

But there was P. Just minutes after Steve had pulled out of the driveway headed for the airport.

P had tried to stay away, he really had. But the pull on him for Rain was too strong. He thought about taking the preppy, fuddy-duddy looking, white-bred muthafuka straight the fuck out! He could have done it quick and easy, too. But Rain was too smart. The only reason he didn't do it first—before approaching Rain? Same reason. She would suspect him the minute she laid eyes on him.

He wished he could have arranged something, a robbery gone bad—*something*--then popped up on her.

Things like that were too risky, though. There wasn't necessarily any guarantee your mark would go down easy and as planned. And if anybody else was involved, for the right amount of money, they would snitch. Or they could get hurt—which P didn't care about. Only problem with having two go down instead of one, is his guy, if he wasn't hurt too bad, would eventually snitch to tha Po-Po's. There was no way a nigga was going to go down severely without getting vengeful if others involved were still around, with no sentences.

P cleared his mind and headed up the steps. He wanted to get on the roof up to the second floor window and surprise her but that would be too much. When she was younger she liked when he did stupid shit like sneaking up on her. But this was her house and she would be freaked out. He felt like he was really close to gaining her trust again—to getting his one wish. He didn't want to do anything to sabotage her from slowly feeling more comfortable with him.

Rain hadn't been feeling too well last night. Partly, she thought, because she wanted Steve to stay home longer. The other part was because of that Subway footlong she ate all by herself. They must have left the mayo out or something because the second she finished it was all over her robe.

This is the second time she has ever called off work.

P rings the bell. Rain, in her ivory silk robe, is upstairs about to get back in bed for an extra hour before her next plan of vegging out in front of the television. When she looks out from the foyer and sees him at the door she steps back from the curtain and ignores him.

He leaves eventually without ringing again. But the next day she goes to work and P calls her and gets Ronya. He tells Ronya Rain has to meet him at the Riverwalk for real.

It is cold weather now but she still goes to meet him.

He goes for it. He grabs her face and kisses her right then and there. It is just like it had been all the other times before—before the guys came busting in and busted their world apart. That same excitable feeling from before. The good times, the good days. Equal desires.

When she pulls away he knows to follow her. To wait a couple of footsteps behind and to get in the truck when she turns a sharp left.

She pulles in the garage of her brownstone but never invites him in. Instead they twist and heave and sweat in the front and back seat of her car. His Brawn, the tattoo of her name seared into his stomach—the way his love feels the same only stronger… It all entices her rather fiercely without shame.

Passion weaves itself between them three--almost four times. The first two times go so fast, had she not heard good pussy did that to a man, she would have been mad.

But the third time……… The third time it is so excruciatingly slow, the ardor—she can still feel the effervesce of their connection residing deep within her.

Would Steve love her enough to stay if it wasn't his? How would she know until it was time? P was so dark the whole thing would surely arouse suspicion. She wanted her marriage—that wasn't up for debate. Steve had only ever been good to her.

Months later she will have all this to think about when the weight is undeniable in her face. Still unnoticeable to anyone other than her—so she thinks.

Steve is merely waiting for her to tell him the good news. The peanut butter and onion fetish she swallows incessantly on weekends in front of *Lifetime or TLC* when Steve is gone. The flutters she would like to one day hold in her arms…

As she sits on that same bench during lunch, as Steve's call follows Perrondre's, there would be a terminal decision to make.

There is a great chance the final decision might come too late.

Like Garden Eyes

The Ruse's Veneration

Camilla is waiting on hands and knees, goose bumped, naked bare body with only a dog collar and leash on. Four minutes later the garage door opens. Ronald drives his truck inside and waits a little, allows the anticipation to build. It's been three years now but each and every time it still feels like the first.

Knowing Ronald is about to open the door makes Camilla's pussy tingle in the best way. When he finally gets out of his truck and opens the door Camilla immediately bends her head and kisses and licks Ronald's shoes.

"Did your master tell you you could touch his shoes?" Ronald shouts at Camilla's bended head. Camilla says nothing. "You may answer," Ronald adds.

"No, master. I'm sorry."

Ronald takes hold of the leash and walks Camilla who is still on her hands and knees to the bathroom. He takes off his suit jacket and unzips his pants.

"Make this dick hard you fuckin' whore!" Ronald yells at a naked Camilla.

She allows him to slide his flaccid penis into her mouth. Ronald starts choking her.

Camilla and Ronald's boss Kenneth who, a few years back made partner at their law firm, has been watching the whole time. "Make her take it all the way down her throat," Kenneth barely whispers from the bathroom doorway. Ronald does just what his boss asks and Camilla sucks until Ronald is at his full eight inches. Ronald is rough and forces himself down Camilla's throat rather harshly, which makes their boss cum in his pants without touching himself.

When she looks like she can't breathe anymore, Ronald pulls on the leash for her to get into the tub where he finishes all over her breasts.

Next Ronald and their boss do double penetration on Camilla. Their boss pulls out and licks around Ronald's dick surrounded by Camilla's wet pussy.

At first Ronald hated that part. Now he has become indifferent to his boss' unconventional ploys.

Some hustle in the streets, for that lean, green, paper money while the office caliber hustle for power and a chance to matriculate from the cubicle to the corner office. Different levels...higher glass ceiling...but it's still the same game.

Once Ronald lays Camilla on her back against the cold bathroom tub and eases out of her tight wet pussy, he cums again, this time all over her clit, which makes Camilla cum hard. Their boss finishes by tonguing all Ronald's cum off Camilla.

Camilla takes a shower with her boss watching and puts on the Chanel suit she wore earlier to the office.

Once they all are dressed, she joins Ronald and her boss in his large, modernly decorated living room that looks like it came from a movie or modern house magazine where they watch *Jeopardy* and dispute each other on the answers.

Camilla's husband calls twice.

On the third call Camilla finally answers. "Hi, honey, how are you? What are the kids up to?" she asks.

"Everyone's fine. What time are you coming home? I have a lot of work to catch up on. I just finished dinner—the kids are eating without you. We go over this every Wednesday and Thursday," he complains. "Can't you ask your boss to allow you to do some of your work from home?"

"I've been trapped in the office as usual. I'll leave right now, honey. If I could get work done from home I would."

"…Well, I love you," her husband says knowing his wife brings in more than he does. It bothers him. He's always the one at the Parent Conference meetings, volley ball games and cello recitals with excuses for why Camilla can never come. If he had it his way she would be a housewife. But Camilla loves being a lawyer and would divorce him quick, fast in a hurry if he dared ask her to quit all together.

And he already knows, even though he makes half of what Camilla makes, she would finagle a way to get him on alimony and child support one way or another. She was a beast in the court of law.

"Love you, too," Camilla adds before tapping end call on her phone.

Ronald's wife has called only once but Ronald ignored her.

"Well, I'll see you guys tomorrow," Camilla says as she raises off the couch and stretches. "I'll be in late...I have court tomorrow," she adds more to Ronald than her boss.

From the first day Ronald joined the law firm Camilla felt connected to him. She thought he needed a haircut but other than that everything about him drove her crazy.

With Ronald, everything was perfect about Camilla the minute he laid eyes on her. But his wife had been his college sweetheart. Everything about Ronald's wife was perfect except the fact that she was a goody-goody. He tried sublimating the things he would like to try in the bedroom with Melissa but it was to no avail. She wasn't having anything of it, winced at the thought of putting her mouth on his dick, refused to allow him to go down on her and made him brush his teeth before he could even think of kissing her.

A year into their escapades, their boss had caught Camilla and Ronald in Ronald's office late one night. The only thing he demanded was to watch. Ronald found it a little odd in the beginning but Camilla hadn't seemed to mind, which pissed Ronald off initially. But Christmas bonuses were great and their boss covered well for them the time Ronald's wife became suspicious and hired a private detective.

Young, Futile Old Girl

Every time Hannah sniffs heroine it adds age to her face. At first she was a very pretty, strawberry haired with smooth, baby-like, wrinkle-free, slightly tanned skin and a slamming body. She could have easily been the feature in a back in the day Playboy spread. Now, as her sniffing habit increases, the twenty-year old looks like a frail, fifty-something. The wrinkles on her face are like waves and ripples of water when she smiles. And she smiles a lot now—thanks to her newfound friend, heroine. She has a habit of rubbing the powder on her lips from time to time. Then she licks her lips in a certain fashion as if to show satisfaction.

The Kaminski family is at their wits end with Hannah. At first no one could tell. It was odd when Hannah refused to go on the yearly family trip to Paris. But they thought she was just being a little rebellious. Maybe she had some new boyfriend she didn't want to leave or maybe she just didn't want to be around them. Then Hannah had dropped all her classes when she was at school in California and she asked to work at the family hardware store in Michigan instead. When she came to work she would go to the break room and nod off to sleep. Add to that hundreds of dollars would come up short at night during cash out. Then Gideon the kitten her mother had just rescued from a tree was missing along with the Bichon Frise and Lab dogs they had had in the family for six years. Hannah had no explanation as to what had happened to any of them even though she was the only one home that day.

When they finally figured out exactly what was up with Hannah they were shocked. How could someone with a 4.0 GPA all her blessed life become an addict? They had given her the world! So they put her in rehab. The best they could find. A quaint little place in San Frisco that was expensive as heck. The center had an excellent reputation.

Even so, Hannah lasted all of three days. She had smooth talked her way out of there and was on a mission for even more heroine.

Her father has followed her and tracked down her dealer and asked him to stop selling to her. A tall, grimy black, ruthless guy who was posted in Detroit in one of the worst neighborhoods in the nation. The dealer broke her father's arm. Mr. Kaminski was lucky that was all the dealer did to him.

Hannah's sister and brother are done with her. They refuse to speak to her even though they live in the same home. She has betrayed them. They used to look up to Hannah; she was their big sis. She was the one they ran to in the middle of the night when they were scared of the Boogie Man and Freddie Krueger. Now she avoided them and had stolen their flat screen televisions out of their rooms.

Her mother has stopped working at the family hardware store in order to watch Hannah around the clock and to prayerfully stop Hannah from stealing everything in the house.

Hannah had been kicked out of her apartment when her roommate became sick of her regular bad behavior and addiction so the family took her in.

It never ceases to amaze Hannah's mother how cunning her daughter is. She sneaks out when her mother falls asleep. Hannah has a trick up her sleeve her mother hasn't figured out yet; she trades her mother's high blood pressure medicine with a sleeping pill. And the sleeping pills knock Mrs. Kaminski out.

Her mother has tabulated all the items and money Hannah has taken from them and subtracted it from her inheritance but Hannah doesn't care. For Hannah each sniff knocks out the pain.

The pain Henry brought on when he cheated on Hannah with her college roommate Heather. What a lame bitch! All the chick did was stay in and study for her freakin' poli-sci classes. Heather still wore panties with the days of the week on them for goodness sake! How could Henry choose Heather over her?

The drug knocked out the pain of her psychology teacher flirting with her. Professor Blackwell was so old he probably passed dust for gas. But that didn't stop him from asking Hannah to stay after class. He had groped her twice and rubbed her face against his penis in his pants. He made her promise not to tell and said he would flunk her is she so much as thought about telling. "Besides," he had said, "No one will believe you!"

Now, thanks to heroine, men no longer look at Hannah in awe. Men like Professor Blackwell and Henry no longer give her a second and third glance.

None of that matters any longer anyhow. Hannah thinks she is at peace. The pain is no longer in her heart. She wears it on her face now.

Soon Mr. and Mrs. Kaminski will have to kick Hannah out. There is nothing else they can do until Hannah wants to stop. She will be the dirty, mangy girl you see at the intersection or strip mall begging for change and food.

The Cult

"One More Push! Come on, Sister Love, PUSH! The baby's head is crowning, you're almost there!" the midwife shouts at Esther in the compound's birthing room.

"I can't! I can't!" Esther Hadassah Love faintly whispers barely able to breathe thru the pain.

"You HAVE to push, Sister!" the midwife's assistant, nineteen year old Sister Mary Exodus yells breaking her silence. She hadn't uttered a word for the last hour. Mary Exodus stands like a mannequin next to the medical bed Ester lays on writhing. Sister Mary Exodus is staring at the pillow elevating Ester's back.

"THAT'S IT! THAT'S IT! The baby is coming!" the midwife shouts relieved.

The baby is crying and so is Esther. She reaches out to hold her new baby girl. The midwife whispers something to Mary Exodus and hands the baby to Mary to clean after the midwife cuts the umbilical cord.

"My baby," Esther says reaching her hands out to Sister Mary Exodus. But the midwife shushes Esther and instead turns around to the cabinet and, after a minute, comes back with a needle concealed from Esther Love.

Two days later, groggy and confused, Esther wakes up out of her drugged state. She is lying in the bed of her two-roomed unit in a flowery housedress she had never seen or worn before. At first she isn't clear where she is or what has just happened.

Sister Mary Exodus comes from the bathroom and hands her a glass of what looks like Coke—something The Laity does not allow. "No. I want my baby. Where is she?" Ester asks the tall, thin brown skinned girl with a tall head wrap just like Esters. Sister Mary Exodus avoids Esther's pleading eyes. "What's going on? My baby—where is she?"

Sister Mary Exodus places the drink on the nightstand next to Ester's twin bed and walks out of the unit.

Esther tries to get up and go into the hallway to find someone who will help her and explain exactly what is going on.

She had been invited to live on the grounds only five months ago. Prior to that she had been in The Laity for a year and a half. When the Brothers and Sisters of The Laity found out she was pregnant and that her child's father was in the army and had died of a brain aneurysm a week before his deployment in Afghanistan ended, they rallied around her like nothing she had ever experienced. They made Esther feel grateful for such loving support.

DaMarco, her child's father, had warned Esther about The Laity a year after she had joined. At first he thought it was a phase. Two hours a day they had to read a weird version of "Life Rules" they called it instead of a bible. They could only drink water or wine. The women had to wear their hair covered at all times—even in bed. Neither the women nor the men were allowed to shave anywhere. DaMarco thought there were too many rules--that The Laity had begun to encumber her life. But Esther told him the army had rules and that she supported him being a soldier.

He had been in the army when they met. She wanted it to be a deal breaker since she did not understand black people joining the United States Army. But she and DaMarco had had instant chemistry; he was a handsome red head with freckles and he was well read and so passionate about life.

It was a chance meeting that night at the bar. DaMarco had never been to Michigan before. He and a buddy had made the trek from Chicago to meet up with an army friend who was in Ann Arbor visiting family after being deployed in Syria.

Thinking about DaMarco now always makes Esther tremor in sadness.

DaMarco had wanted her to leave the religion alone when she and he had first found out in the doctor's office they were expecting a girl.

But these people were doing the will of God, right? They were always happy and helpful and had created their own safe haven. It had been an environment shielded from the world… And that is what she wanted—for her daughter to grow up in a spiritual purlieu--since the world wa becoming worse and worse.

Maybe I just don't understand what is going on, she thinks.

Esther makes an attempt to get up once again. Sharp pains shoot throughout her. She feels dizzy. *I have to, for DaMarco and Eden!* She reminds herself.

Finally she stands up and walks into the hallway. The loud speaker is blasting prayer. People, the Brothers and Sisters at the other end of the hallway, are standing still with their heads bent listening. None of that matters at this moment. All Esther can think of are DaMarco and her new baby girl, Eden.

"PLEASE, WHERE IS THE MIDWIFE?" she asks Brother Lazarus as she stumbles her way down the hallway.

He does not answer her. He just continues listening to the prayer. Prayer usually takes five minutes.

Esther falters past Brother Lazarus and slowly makes her way to the elevator. She reaches the first floor and makes her way to the receptionist desk. "Hello, Sister Matthews. Do you know where the midwife is?" She asks.

The receptionist does not move her bent head to acknowledge Esther.

Esther is so unstable she feels as though she will fall. She begins to crawl her way towards the exit of the compound so that she can go to the medical office in the other building.

Once outside in the parking lot, a security guard spots Esther on her knees crawling. "GO BACK, NOW, SISTER!" he shouts at her but she does not listen. He calls on his phone for backup and, as slowly as Esther is moving, it is easy for the extra security to catch her.

"WHAT ARE YOU DOING?" the other officer asks her.

"MY BABY—WHERE IS SHE?" she asks.

"You can't leave your unit until dinner," he responds never intending to answer Esther.

"I have to find my baby," Esther states.

"LOOK! GO BACK OR ELSE!" the first security guard warns.

Esther continues to crawl along the sidewalk. She shouts and cries out for help a few steps away from the front of the compound's dorms when she sees the backup security guard pulling out his taser gun. He zaps Esther. She loses control of her body.

The first security guard bends over and picks Esther off the sidewalk. She lies like a caught fish in the arms of the guard.

Once back in her unit in the compound, security arranges for a security apprentice, twenty-year old Brother David Solomon, to watch Esther.

"Here's dinner," Brother David Solomon says handing Esther a tray of organic chicken breasts, corn on the cob and cabbage all grown on the grounds farm.

"I just want my baby," Esther replies placing the food next to the Coke-like, liquid substance Sister Mary Exodus, Brother David Solomon's fiancé, had placed on the nightstand earlier.

"Well, if you do what God wants, maybe The Queen Mother will come visit you," he offers.

Esther Love's motherly instinct kicks in even stronger. He is the only person that has answered anything she has said all day. "What should I do to get a visit from The Queen Mother?" Esther asks.

"Run with God's flow and let go," he answers.

"Can you please tell The Queen Mother I'd like to speak with her?" Esther asks more than eager.

"It's not up to me but I will let The Officials know of your request," Brother David Solomon responds.

"Look, you and Sister Mary Exodus will be getting married next month, right?" Esther pushes at the opportunity.

"Yes."

"Well, just imagine when you two have a baby. You'll be so happy. You will want to love and protect that small human. You will want it to have the best and most of all to be loved. Just imagine that. How would you feel if your baby had been ripped away from you—and if you didn't even get to hold that baby in your arms and let your offspring feel your tender touch? I'm not asking for much—I will do whatever The Laity asks of me. I just want my baby—my little girl. That's it." She hopes she has softened his heart.

Brother David Solomon receives a text. His face scrunches. "I'll be back," he tells Esther and leaves her unit.

At first, Esther thinks she has pushed too hard. But upon second thought, she knows she must do whatever it takes to find Eden quickly.

Everyone is at dinner. She is still shaky but better able to stand. She doesn't even take the time out to put on shoes. She locks the bathroom door and closes it to make it seem as if she is in there and slips out of the room into the hallway and out of the building undetected this time, thank God.

The Queen Mother and her husband, The King of The Laity eat before everyone else so maybe, if she goes to her courtyard in the third building, she will find her and will be able to get her help in finding Eden.

It's easier than Esther expected to get into the courtyard. The guards are watching ESPN (which is against The Program of Commandments; the Brothers and Sisters are not allowed to watch cable). Lucky for Esther the guards are not paying any attention to her as she sneaks inside.

The top floor is the courtyard. Esther is about to press the top floor, the fifth floor, but quickly decides to go to the fourth floor since the elevator leads directly into The Queen Mother and The King of The Laity's loft style apartment. Once she is on the fourth floor, she finds the stairwell. In seconds she finds the entry to the fifth floor and it is wedged open with a stack of The Laity's newspapers. Instinct demands she lie low and be as inconspicuous as possible in the hallway.

She cracks the door open a little wider and immediately Esther sees the midwife in the living room with a small infant. Her back is turned away from the entrance of the loft and she is cooing at the fussy baby and singing to her. *That's MY baby,* Esther thinks feeling the breastmilk in her began to flow.

When the midwife walks to another room Esther crawls inside and hides behind a sectional couch.

"He's hungry, I think," the midwife walks back into the living room and tells The Queen Mother.

Wait a minute, HE? That's not my baby, Esther thinks panicking. *Where is MY baby?*

Queen Mother is in the dinning room with a nail tech polishing her shellac nails. "I just had more formula special delivered yesterday. It's supposed to be the best out. Go in the kitchen and look in the cabinet over the microwave. You should see it there."

"Ok, I'll get it," the midwife says. When she comes back from the kitchen, which is four times larger than Esther's unit she adds, "Aww, he has red hair--he's so adorable. Thank God, Esther didn't start breastfeeding him. He'd never take formula after that."

"Come sit with me," The Queen Mother tells the midwife. The Queen Mother is drinking wine and motions for the midwife to pour herself a glass. "It's a four hundred dollar wine and is it ever good!" she laughs.

In between sips of wine, the midwife feeds Esther's son.

Esther waits them out. The nail tech leaves.

After almost two hours of talking about more rules to add to The Program of Commandments and wine, The Queen Mother retires to her bedroom while the midwife places the baby in the bassinette and falls asleep on the couch.

This is Esther's only chance and she knows it.

She makes her way to the bassinette and scoops the baby into her arms. She walks to the elevator and changes her mind. Instead she takes the back stairs she came from. *Ok, baby. You've got to stay asleep. Mommy's got you,* she thinks.

Once Esther gets on the first floor of the stairwell she realizes she will have to exit where the guards are. She is scared to open the door to assess them and figure out how to escape the guards unnoticed.

She cracks the door open to see one guard eating and the other still glued to the television. She decides the time is not right. She will have to wait them out as well.

Not knowing how long it's been she cracks the door open again only to see two new guards at the front desk. Shift change. She waits and waits—it feels like she will be waiting forever. But as long as the baby is still asleep, Esther feels as though she has a chance.

Finally, when Esther cracks the door open, both guards are gone. She makes a break for it. She goes to the exit area and finds another door, a back entrance. She leaves out. Her heart is beating wickedly. She can barely breath. *Baby, please don't wake up just yet! Please help me, God!*

The compound and farm are at least ten acres combined. The fact that it is August and still warm out works in Esther's favor. She realizes she will have to walk thru the farm to get to the road. Her feet are throbbing and bleeding but that doesn't matter. The baby has made a few little noises and that is what is worrying her.

She walks low in the cornfields trying not to be spotted. The cornfield is the only area not gated. It leads to the road. She knows because it has been her work assignment for the last four and a half months; she has had to work twelve hours, six days a week in the cornfields.

She can see the road but it is still some distance away. All of a sudden, she sees flashing lights. She hears a car horn. They are on to her! They call out her name over a loudspeaker. "SISTER LOVE? SISTER LOVE, PLEASE COME BACK!"

Esther begins to run still remaining as low to the ground as possible so security won't have a clear view of her. Finally, she reaches the road. She can see a black car from the compound approaching her thru the field.

She tries to flag down three cars on the road to no avail. When the compound guards are almost six hundred feet away from her the baby awakens and starts crying.

She jumps in the middle of the road.

A red pick up truck stops just a few seconds away from hitting her. "WHAT IN HELL'S TARNATION IS WRONG WITH YOU?" the driver shouts at Esther.

"HELP ME, SIR! PLEASE TAKE ME TO THE HOSPITAL! HELP ME! YOU SEE THAT CAR? THEY'RE AFTER ME!"

But it is too late. Four security guards are directly behind Esther. "COME BACK, SISTER LOVE! YOU HAVE STOLEN THE LAITY'S NEXT PRINCE! YOU ARE TAMPERING WITH THE WILL OF GOD AND YOU WILL NOT BE RECOMMENDED FOR HEAVEN! BLACK PEOPLE NEED THIS PRINCE! "

"THIS IS MY BABY! HELP ME, SIR! TAKE ME TO THE HOSPITAL!" She completely ignores the guards.

The pickup driver is unsure of what to believe or what to do.

Esther senses this and makes him a desperate offer. "If you take me to the hospital, you can stay and see that this is my child. If I am wrong you can bring him back to them. JUST HELP ME PLEASE!!!"

After quickly mulling the situation over, the pickup driver opens the passenger's door and says to Esther, "Ok, git in. There's a hospital near by but they ain't got no maternity ward, I don't reckon. I'll take you to Kalamazoo. It's 'bout thirty minutes."

One of The Laity's security guards grabs Esther's right arm where her son lies and tells her, "You can go but the boy must stay!"

Esther hops in the truck with her crying son. "Thank you, sir!" Esther turns to the skinny, white Santa look-a-like pickup driver and says, "They took my son from me!"

Another one of The Laity's guards reaches for the door and tries to pull Esther out of the truck.

"GIT! I SAID GIT!" The driver says before adding, "I have a license to carry and I ain't scared to pull one out on ya!"

At that, security backs away and retreats from the pickup truck, Esther and the baby.

"I ain't never liked those niggers being down here in Paw Paw anyhow—they need to go back to Detroit," the driver informs Esther. Realizing Esther is black too he recants, "Not all of 'em are bad, you know. Just these bunch don't seem like they up to no good."

"Thank you for picking us up. You saved our lives."

"Yeah, well, something had to be wrong fer ya to almost kill yaself on a road."

Esther looks down at the baby in her arms and looks into her baby's face. She smiles thru her tears. "It was worth it to have this little guy in my arms right now." The Laity has him swaddled in black cotton and with a black triangular hat on his head.

"What just happened?" the driver asks Esther.

Esther explains the last three days to the driver and tells him about DaMarco.

"Wow! I knew them people weren't no good! My name is Ernie, by the way."

"I'm Andrea—Andrea Mathis," she says.

"Well, the Good Lord was watching over you and ya boy! He come from good stock, army dad and all," Ernie adds.

When they get to the hospital, Andrea and her baby are admitted in the emergency to both be examined.

Ernie calls his wife and lets her know of his strange encounter and that he will be staying at the hospital for a little while longer to make sure Andrea and the baby are ok.

Due to the bizarre circumstances, a DNA test is administered. DaMarco Junior is for a certainty Andrea Mathis' son and he is healthy. Andrea was worried they may have done something to him.

A social worker visits Andrea the following day and helps her find aftercare for she and Junior. Andrea had given up her clerical job of five years with the IRS to be a full-time Laity member.

A women's center in Ann Arbor is willing to take Andrea's case and help her get on her feet. But Andrea does not want to be in Michigan near the people of The Laity ever again.

DaMarco's mother lives in Georgia. The social worker helps her reach out to her. Once released from the hospital, Andrea goes to live with his mother and to start a new life.

Ishia

There is always a chick like her no matter where you go.

They say spirits never die, that they only transmute themselves into new candidates. Ishia is no longer a new candidate but definitely one of the feared spirits now.

For the time being, she works at the cursed spa in the mall that is in need of a heavy exorcism. In a year she'll be working at a bank and then who knows where three months later after she quits the humdrum of the financial gig.

At the time she is a nail tech—the one who sits quietly minding her own business. Her clientele is off the chains. Seems like everyone coming in there only wants Ishia to do their full sets and to mend their broken tips.

Ishia is a different looking black woman: excruciatingly pale almost white skin toned with a round, wide forehead and odd eyes that look like purple contacts from a distance. Close up you can tell they are brown. But there's something about those eyes; they look dark and distant after you figure out she isn't wearing a pair of odd colored fake ones. Even when she is with a client and engrossed in deep conversation, her naturally purpled stain lips tell you they are holding back; that they have crossed over.

It all started when her girlfriend Jazzy, a stripper, told Ishia that Ishia's husband Damon was up in her club. This is the reason now in most Michigan based titty bars women cannot come in unless they are accompanied by a male.

Ishia went to the club the following week and sat and watched. At first her husband, who was at this point a regular, didn't notice. But eventually her eyes burned thru the extra thick chick who was the exact opposite of Ishia's svelt, skinny catwalk frame.

Well, her husband snuck out of the club when he spotted Ishia.

The stripper girl was the kind that went to church at 10 am right after charging a regular $250 at 5 am for her pussy in the parking lot of the gas station next to the strip joint.

She was grinding on top of Ishia's husband.

Ishia went to her husband's car and, since the dummy hadn't locked the doors, opened one and smacked the stripper girl and him.

Ishia ran from her husband's car before he had a chance to react and got in the car with Passion—her then best friend (she ended up sleeping with Passion shortly after this event with her husband Damon).

Passion was the one that introduced Ishia to Jazzy and the world of strippers. Passion who, after getting divorced and turning into a thirty-one year old who had dated almost every twenty-one year old thing slinging a dick in Detroit, was secretly happy Ishia was leaving Damon. The way Passion saw it, now they could live together and hang out more.

But Ishia's revenge is deeper than that. She has moved to an apartment in West Bloomfield and, although she can sometimes barely make rent, when Damon comes over to pick up their daughter and begs her back she is slightly happy with that.

But that is still not her true revenge on Damon for cheating on her with that fat ass stripper.

Now, good girl turned tarot card reader has infected all the other girls at the spa with such things. She knows ahead of time whether or not a client will be late. Whether or not Damon will call that night. All on account of her Fairy cards and her crystal pendulum.

She hides it well. Currently she is dating a real ratchet preacher who kind of looks like an oversized Johnny Gill. But he isn't much of a preacher. He's given her two STD's to date.

When she finally escapes Obese Johnny Gill, she meets a dark skinned gorgeous city worker. But he is crazy. He stands outside her apartment window and throws stuff when she doesn't answer his calls. And he is a cheater. He is forty and playing Ishia with some woman named Ernestine who is fifty-four and pays his phone bill and car note.

This next one she really likes is Edward. But he barely helps her on the bills and she is about to get put out of her suburb apartment.

Ishia resorts to sleeping with the old white owner of her apartment building but that only works for so long. He has given her furniture for her place but since she isn't willing to comply with his daddy/daughter fantasies he is pretty much done.

She even pushed a girl she worked with at the spa, an esthetician named Bianca, on the apartment owner. Bianca is pretty, smart enough and married but separated. But Bianca only works out for one month's worth of rent in February.

It is now April.

Although they talked for a few weeks on the phone, Bianca had only gone on one date with the apartment owner and she wouldn't kiss his asymmetrical dentures.

Bianca and Ishia fall out after Ishia gives the scoop on Bianca's sexual encounters with another guy to Bianca's estranged husband.

Bianca just doesn't understand why Ishia would do that to her. Ishia has even tried to get Bianca to escort with her and a Transvestite named Wonder.

After she falls out with Jazzy and Passion and now having nowhere to go and, after all the hoeing to pay Damon back, Ishia agrees to move back in with her husband. He's been asking her to come back home for the last two years.

Besides her daughter needs some type of stable home. At this point Ishia's worked six different jobs and her daughter has switched schools three times now in two years. The little girl even talks very properly now—the West Bloomfield school system did that. Her daughter looks like she will one day be a model with all that height and the pre-good looks. But it could go either way because she likes to play basketball and has seen her mother do a few strange things with Passion.

Ishia renews her vows to Damon four months after moving back into his Detroit home. She gives up the sessions with psychics and the fairy cards.

She is now a believer and saved and works at the church.

Like Garden Eyes

Like Garden Eyes

"You are a witch!" The girl's uncle says in their language before spiting on her and continues walking to get water.

She is sitting watching the action around her in her usual spot in the dirt in the center of the village on her knees. This is nothing new. Her mother will soon come out of the shack and smack her for the same reason.

The Catholic priest declared her a witch at birth.

Dark reddish ebony skin, her hair is straw yellow and her eyes are naturally a mix of aqua and penetrating gray.

No one has seen such a thing in these parts. There is no television. Other than what information the Catholic missionaries tell them verbally, literature outside of the bible has not been brought to the people. Not even their country's newspapers are presented to the people. The few that can read in their language are encouraged to only read the bible. But the bible brought to them is English, which presents a problem.

At first her mother breast-fed the strange looking baby and prayed she would eventually change into a more acceptable situation. But after five years of age her mother and father both gave up. They were told by Father that the child was an evil entity sent here to torment her people.

That if they prayed, bathed her in holy water and gave to the church whatever they could manage, she may eventually be converted from a witch to a well person.

They would know she was well when her hair and eyes darkened.

To prove their allegiance to their faith, her family constantly beats her in at the public meeting place. No one feeds her. Many are sure she is a witch because the child manages to still survive. When the village is asleep, she wonders in fear and steals food from their gardens. So far no one except one child has noticed her in their gardens.

Her eyes glowed in such a way, the child was paralyzed with fear and afraid he would be beaten for looking at her.

Other times, when the risks are too great, she eats what she manages from garbages and often steals the water from the chickens and goats.

She is not allowed near the well.

All of the children in the village refuse to go near her. The goats, dogs and cats are not allowed to play with her. The people think she will taint their goat milk or possess their dogs—this is what Father has told them.

Though Father is not the same color as them and his hair is different, it is not gold like hers. A few of the missionaries have eyes similar to hers but Father has told them that it is okay because they are different and sent to help their people. But for the girl, this is unacceptable because she belongs to them and should look like them.

Since age five, the girl has never been hugged. The closes she has come to a loving touch is when one of the missionaries place their hands on her forehead during a Sunday service and asked God to wash away her sins.

Thin, tall and elegant, in another place this girl would be model material; she would be sought out for the very reasons she is taunted here.

The fact that she is not fat is also another problem. At her age, were she considered normal, her mother would be fattening her with goat milk and limiting her physical activity so she would be considered robust and fittingly fat for a husband.

No one will ever marry her. At fourteen girls in this area are usually given in marriage.

Three years away from that, she has managed. But how long she can survive in such a manner is debatable. With no future prospect husband, things do not look good. She does not even know to run away. She could just start walking. This would actually make her family very relieved. They would think God was blessing them if she walked away and never came back.

But there are animals a couple of miles away that would like nothing more than to encounter fresh meat. Unless she chooses the right direction, walking away is the same as staying.

Like Garden Eyes

Other Books

Even If You Don't...
A contemporary romance novel

Everything In Style Should Not Be Worn
Sci Fi, Rants, Poetry Collection

Just Talking To You Because There Is No One Else To Talk To: My Journal & Other Things
Collection #2

Vert Means More Than Green: Very Explicit Real Talk
Astrology, Very Explicit Real Talk

Kamikaze of Songs
Songs, Poetry, Photojournalism, Prose

The Essay Collection
What is Wrong With Black People Today?
What Black Women Need to Know!
For Our Brothas...

Email comments to mianne@mianneAbooks.com

Liked what you read? Please write a review on Amazon or Bn.com
or
email your comments to mianne@mianneAbooks.com

Thanks!

www.ingramcontent.com/pod-product-compliance
Lightning Source LLC
LaVergne TN
LVHW041628060526
838200LV00040B/1484